*Here's what reviewers
are saying about*
TO HAVE AND TO HOLD

"At last a line that goes beyond the 'happily ever after' ending. . . . What really makes these books special is their view of marriage as an exciting, vibrant blossoming of love out of the courtship stage. Clichés such as the 'other woman' are avoided, as family backgrounds are beautifully interwoven with plot to create a very special romantic glow."

—Melinda Helfer, *Romantic Times*

"At last, a series of honest, convincing and delightfully reassuring stories about the joys of matrimonial love. Men and women who sometimes doubt that a happy marriage can be achieved should read these books."

—Vivien Jennings, *Boy Meets Girl*

"I am extremely impressed by the high quality of writing within this new line. Romance readers who have been screaming for stories of romance, sensuality, deep commitment and love will not want to miss this line. I feel that this line will become not only a favorite of mine but of the millions of romance readers."

—Terri Busch, *Heart Line*

"Easy does it, angel."
Rafe chuckled.

"Still think you can take me on, do you?" His tongue flicked over her compressed lips.

"Yes," she gasped, loving every pore in his face, her hand coming up to touch the fading scar on his jawbone where he had been cut in the crash. "You shouldn't lift me the way you do. I'm too heavy, and you're not strong enough yet," she mumbled, not sure what she was saying.

"You're talking gibberish, do you know that?" Rafe muttered, nibbling at her ear.

"Whatever." Cady bit at his chin and his cheekbones, loving the feel of him.

"Are you going to make a meal out of me?"

"Maybe. Do you mind?" Cady felt glazed from head to toe. She felt a sense of triumph that he was as aroused as she by their love play. Maybe she wouldn't be able to keep him forever, she thought, but while she had him she was going to love him.

Dear Reader:

The event we've all been waiting for has finally arrived! The publishers of SECOND CHANCE AT LOVE are delighted to announce the arrival of TO HAVE AND TO HOLD. Here is the line of romances so many of you have been asking for. Here are the stories that take romance fiction into the thrilling new realm of married love.

TO HAVE AND TO HOLD is the first and only romance series that portrays the joys and heartaches of marriage. Its unique concept makes it significantly different from the other lines now available to you. It conforms to a standard of high quality set and maintained by SECOND CHANCE AT LOVE. And, of course, it offers all the compelling romance, exciting sensuality, and heartwarming entertainment you expect in your romance reading.

We think you'll love TO HAVE AND TO HOLD romances—and that you'll become the kind of loyal reader who is making SECOND CHANCE AT LOVE an ever-increasing success. Look for four TO HAVE AND TO HOLD romances in October and three each month thereafter, as well as six SECOND CHANCE AT LOVE romances each and every month. We hope you'll read and enjoy them all. And please keep your letters coming! Your opinion is of the utmost importance to us.

Warm wishes,

Ellen Edwards

Ellen Edwards
TO HAVE AND TO HOLD
The Berkley Publishing Group
200 Madison Avenue
New York, N.Y. 10016

To Have and to Hold

TREAD SOFTLY

ANN CRISTY

A SECOND CHANCE AT LOVE BOOK

Poem quoted from "He Wishes for the Cloths of Heaven," by W. B. Yeats, in *The Wind in the Reeds*. Quoted with permission from A. P. Watts Literary Agents, London, 1982.

TREAD SOFTLY

First edition published October 1983

First printing

Printed in the United States of America

To Have and to Hold books are published by
The Berkley Publishing Group
200 Madison Avenue, New York, NY 10016

I have spread my dreams under your feet;
Tread softly because you tread on my dreams.

—"He Wishes for the Cloths of Heaven,"
by William Butler Yeats

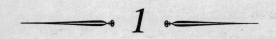

1

CADY LEANED OVER Rafe's sleeping form and kissed his cheek. It had been two months since the operation and soon he would be going home. He could speak, he could walk...Cady shrugged. Well, he could move in his walker a few feet more each day. Soon he would be back to full strength, the doctors assured her, and at his job in the Senate as junior senator from the state of New York. Cady sighed. Maybe she would again find herself in the limbo their marriage had been in before the airplane accident that had cost Rafe so much.

No...Even now, as she watched his eyes flutter, Cady vowed to herself that no one would relegate her to the hidey-hole life she'd been leading before the accident five agonizing months ago, when the plane carrying Rafe and a few friends crashed. They had been on their way to Durra, his father's home in Maryland, named after the tiny hamlet in Ireland where Rafe's great-grandfather was born. The Learjet's engine had malfunctioned; the plane had hit the ground on a wingtip and somersaulted

1

into a tree. The pilot had been killed, and Rafe, who had been standing talking to his friends, had broken his back, causing a vertebra to press on his spinal column. He'd been paralyzed from the neck down as a result. He'd received further damage from a severe blow to the head when his body was flung through the cabin. His vocal cords had been injured, but, although at first the doctors were not hopeful about Rafe's back, they'd been confident he would at least regain control of his voice.

When Dr. Kellman had come forward and told Cady his feeling that with a radical type of surgery with which he had previously been successful, Rafe would again be mobile, Cady had felt the beginning of hope.

"The spine would be fused here...here...here..." Dr. Kellman pointed to the many dots on the scan. "Admittedly, the more points of injury, the greater the risk." The doctor stared at her, his mouth tight. "But I also feel that his chances are very good. Of course, there will be long weeks of physical therapy, speech therapy..." The surgeon tapped his pointer on the desk. "But with the use of the 'Halo,' the head device I described to you that will keep him immobile, I think we'll succeed."

Cady stood and shook Dr. Kellman's hand. "Doctor, thank you." She took a deep breath. "I'd like time to think this over, and of course I'll consult with other specialists."

Cady's research had confirmed what Dr. Kellman told her. There had been success with such a procedure, but it was still experimental, radical, and because so many pressure points on the spine were involved, very risky indeed. Still, when Rafe had not responded to physical therapy or to any of the other types of treatment the doctors had tried, it became clear that the only hope for his full recovery lay in the new laser surgery that Dr. Kellman recommended.

As she watched the vacant look in Rafe's blue eyes as he came awake, the restless flutter of his hands as he clutched at the covering sheet, Cady remembered the long days in the nursing cottage when his eyes were the only moving part on that vital form. It still made her shudder with pain to think of it. She recalled the day she had told him she was going ahead with the operation, over the strong opposition of his father.

"Emmett is furious that I would dare contemplate having such a radical procedure performed on you." Cady lifted the flaccid hand to her mouth, delighting in being able to touch him. "Oh, I know it's because he fears for your life." She smiled at her husband, kissing each of his fingers. "He would rather have you confined to this Stryker frame than risk your life." She had watched his blue eyes become cobalt rays burning into her mind. "Oh, yes, I know how you feel about that. I have no intention of letting anyone interfere with the surgery that Dr. Kellman feels can help you." Cady caught her breath as the fire deepened in his eyes. For a moment she felt as though he were speaking to her rather than blinking his eyes, as he usually did to communicate.

She cleared her throat. "Ah...the governor called this morning and asked if I would consider running for your seat if you're unable to do so." She rubbed Rafe's limp hand against her cheek, wanting to touch him. "I told him I would be busy campaigning for you." She kneaded his hand gently.

Before his accident, she and Rafe had been estranged for nearly five years. They had lived in the same house but almost as strangers. It hadn't been a cataclysmic schism but rather a gradual alienation that had begun with Cady's dislike of some of her father-in-law's friends. To her, these people seemed like leeches trying to suck the vitality from Rafe's high-level priorities and leave behind the sleazy money-making schemes they represented. Rafe had defended his father's cronies and insisted that he had to give careful consideration to the bills that many of them urged him to support. His sheepish defense of these people during heated arguments with Cady had bordered on the defensive, she thought in retrospect. At the time, however, she had interpreted Rafe's hesitation as a sign that he was on the verge of knuckling under to his father's friends' demands. She had been bitter in her denunciations of these men—and of her husband for listening to them.

More and more Rafe had attended parties alone, especially the parties his father gave at Durra. True, he had initially asked Cady to attend these gatherings with him. She had refused, partly because of her dislike of Emmett Densmore, Rafe's father, who had never accepted Cady as his son's wife. But the parties at Durra were a sore point with Cady for another reason as well.

It wasn't so much the scandal that had broken when Rafe, then a freshman congressman, had been discovered hosting a private party at Durra where the only guests other than men in public office had been a bevy of notorious call girls. After all, the episode had occurred before Cady had even met her future husband. But Rafe had never mentioned the incident, had indeed acted as if the parties at his father's estate were dull, staid political affairs, and he had been lukewarm in his urging that Cady accompany him. Diffidently he had offered to forgo them himself, though Cady, unwilling to create a wedge between father and son, wouldn't hear of it. Yet she couldn't help wondering if her husband's silence about the scandal and his continued presence at what she could only speculate were little better than orgies weren't proof that he had not forsaken the wild playboy life that he had led prior to their marriage. Hints to this effect from Bruno Trabold, Emmett Densmore's most intimate assistant and manager of his various sidelines and investments, fueled Cady's suspicions. But pride—and love—prevented her from confronting Rafe about the parties at Durra.

As time went on it seemed that Rafe spent more and more time at his father's estate. Cady sought to fill the lonely hours by enrolling at Georgetown University to pursue a master's degree in archaeology. She was encouraged in this endeavor by Rafe's colleague, Rob Ardmore, a young congressman from Iowa. Rob also suggested that Cady do her utmost to combat what he suggested was an undue influence over Rafe of his father's questionable associates. But Rafe seemed to turn a deaf ear to everything she said. While she studied, he partied. The rift between husband and wife widened.

"I suppose you'd rather I didn't even sleep in this room," Rafe had said to her one evening when he walked into their bedroom and she grabbed a dressing gown and held it up in front of her.

"That's up to you," Cady had responded coldly.

Rafe had moved into another bedroom the next day, tearing Cady apart, though she had said nothing to dissuade him.

She had held her breath waiting for him to ask for a divorce. Days went by when she didn't even see him. She had been glad to take a trip back to New York State to see her father in the university town of Ithaca.

It was while she was there that the call had come informing her of the accident. "It's Rafe." Emmett didn't spare her. "The plane crashed on the way to Durra. He's alive, but it's bad. Get here fast." The phone had crashed down, leaving Cady to arrange her return trip to Washington. She had felt as though her insides were shredded. She remembered being on the plane and thinking Rafe mustn't die. She had promised an elusive deity that she would do anything if only her husband's life were spared.

She studied Rafe again as he came more fully awake.

"Hello. You had a long, deep sleep." Cady felt her smile slip sideways under Rafe's long scrutiny.

"Hello," he answered, his voice retaining the slight hoarseness that the doctors assured her would gradually fade. "It always seems as though I'm still unable to speak when I first awaken." He swallowed. "God, it was awful having to blink my eyes to communicate." His mouth lifted at the corners. "Sometimes I think you read my mind rather than my blinks." He coughed and nodded gratefully when Cady held out the water mug with the bent glass straw. Rafe took several deep drafts, sighing and leaning back against the pillows. "I'll never forget that helicopter ride from the nursing cottage to here. I wanted either to be well again or to die on the operating table."

Cady could feel the pressure of tears building in her eyes. "I knew how you felt."

Rafe turned his head on the pillow. "I know you did. And I appreciate your standing up to my father when he tried to block the surgery. I could blink my consent, but the operation wouldn't have been properly authorized without your having signed the release papers. Dad would have used all his influence to prevent it if you hadn't kept it secret from him until after I was already on the operating table."

Cady shuddered in reminiscence of her father-in-law's ire when he had discovered that his son was in the midst of undergoing the experimental surgery. "Emmett was furious with me," she said quietly.

"Don't I know it!" Rafe grinned at her, some of the pallor leaving his haggard face. "And I can imagine how you felt when my brothers arrived to visit me less than an hour before the helicopter was scheduled to take me from the nursing home to the National Institutes of Health for the operation."

Cady grazed her knuckles across her lips and nodded, recalling her shock when the twins, Rafe's brothers, had ambled into the cottage. She had frowned at them in her fear. "What are you doing here? I thought you visited Rafe earlier in the day."

"Nice greeting, Cady," Gareth, the more voluble twin, offered before going over to the bed and lifting Rafe's heavy arm. "I bet you didn't expect to see me twice in one day, did you, old man?" Gareth said to Rafe. "Gavin decided he would come after practice because he had a makeup test today. So I came with him." The sandy-haired giant turned around to look at Cady. "Satisfied, o sister-in-law who never smiles anymore?"

"Hey, Gareth, knock it off. Cady smiles. She's just tired from working those long hours in Rafe's Senate office," the lesser giant with the darker-color hair answered, smiling in his rather shy way at Cady before walking toward the hospital bed and grinning at his brother. In the quick, restrained way he had, Gavin leaned down to kiss his brother on the cheek.

Cady liked the twins, although at times she thought Gareth a little too flippant and outspoken. It was enough for her that they came to visit Rafe. That made them top drawer to Cady. She cleared her throat, wondering how she was going to get rid of them. "Ah . . . I . . . ah . . . this . . . I hate to say that this is my hour, but it is." She looked at a now-frowning Gareth, her eyes steady.

"Cady of the tiny slim body, the honey-color hair, and the violet eyes that should have been fawn-brown to go with the rest of your coloring. You surprise me, as usual. Why do you want us to go? You always seem to be in there battling about something, but you look as fragile as that Belleek china from Ireland that Dad prizes so much. What's going on behind that doll face, Cady?" Gareth quizzed her, his careless college look fading into a sharp-eyed study.

His twin glanced up from Rafe's bed. His quiet eyes had an arrested look as the color rose in Cady's face.

"Why does it seem strange to you that I would want my designated hour alone with my husband? It wasn't my idea to break the time down so that Emmett and Bruno could have their special times." She bit her lip as she heard her voice rise in a hysterical way. At all costs she had to keep her cool. Nothing must be allowed to interfere with Rafe being taken to the hospital today and operated on by Dr. Kellman. All the plans hinged on split-second timing. If Rafe's father ever suspected, he would try to stop her.

Graf's low growl seemed to steady Cady's nerves. She was grateful that Rafe had requested, through blinks, to have their chocolate-brown Doberman pinscher with him in the nursing cottage. Even Albert Trock, the male nurse who was Rafe's constant attendant at the nursing home, thought the dog was good for Rafe's morale.

Both Gareth and Gavin looked at the Doberman curled next to the bed.

"Why the hell do you bring Graf every time you come, Cady?" Gareth asked, scowling amusement as the large dog stretched. "He doesn't seem to like anyone but you and Rafe."

"I like him," Gavin announced, approaching the Doberman but not touching him. Graf looked back at him in unblinking appraisal. "He has a dignity about him, a sense of worth."

Cady laughed, so relieved that the subject had been changed that she could feel the moisture beading on her upper lip. "Yes, Dobermans seem to have that look about them. That's why I call him Graf, meaning 'count' in German. He's a gentle dog, but he's also very protective of Rafe, so he doesn't unbend with anyone when he's here." Cady paused for a moment. "Though that's not quite true. There's a nurse here named Trock, and Graf seems to like him. Trock's marvelous with Rafe—they even play chess together, with Rafe blinking to show the moves he wants to make on the chessboard." She smiled at the twins, not happy that she had to resist disclosing what would be happening to Rafe that very day. But she couldn't risk Bruno Trabold or Emmett Densmore's interference. She fully intended to tell all of them, but not until the operation began.

It was a stroke of luck when Gavin reminded his garrulous twin of the beer blast on their dorm floor at Georgetown that evening. In short order they informed their immobile brother of all the lurid events that would no doubt take place, then took themselves off, laughing and promising to return the next day.

The guilty feelings that Cady experienced at keeping such a secret from the twins lessened when Dr. Kellman called her from Bethesda.

"We're ready for him, Cady. How are things at your end?"

"Good so far. I've just heard from one of the nurses

that the helicopter is standing by. No one is too suspicious because I had informed the staff that I had a meeting that would necessitate the use of a helicopter." Cady shuddered. "Dr. Kellman, I'm so afraid. I know I'm doing the right thing. It's hell for Rafe to be a prisoner in his own body, but I'm afraid of losing him, too." She looked at Rafe when she spoke, feeling his eyes fixed on her. There was a blue-flame message there. "Of course I'm going through with it . . . but I'm frightened."

When she had completed the call, she remembered now, she had walked back to Rafe's bed to talk to him. "It won't be long now. I'm just waiting for the shift to change. We'll go when the early-shift doctors have left and the others are making rounds in the far wing." She had smiled down at him. "I feel as though we're caught in the middle of a spy film." Cady had sunk into the chair, holding Rafe's limp hand to her forehead.

Later that day, as she had waited outside the operating room for progress reports on Rafe, she had at last braved the face-to-face encounter with Emmett Densmore that she'd been dreading.

Bruno Trabold in tow, Emmett strode down the corridor to where Cady waited, his eyes blazing with wrath. "You tricked me," he accused. "And you enlisted the aid of that man Trock to lie to me, to stall me, so that I wouldn't know that Rafe had been transferred here for surgery until it was too late to do anything about it." He gave her a look of sheer hatred. "If my son dies," he hissed menacingly, "his death will be on your head."

Cady gasped, closed her eyes for a moment, then forced her gaze to meet Emmett's unwaveringly. "I'm doing what Rafe wants," she said levelly. "What we both want. I'm sorry that deception was necessary, Emmett, but my husband's wishes come before yours—or even my own. It's his life, after all."

"His death will be on your head," her father-in-law repeated ominously.

"He's not going to die! And he's not going to live out his life as a vegetable, either! The operation will succeed, and Rafe will be reelected to the Senate in November," Cady said, her words more a prayer than an expression of certainty.

"Will he?" Bruno Trabold mocked her. "What if he's not around to be reelected in November, Acting Senator Densmore?" His voice dripped venom. "Then I guess you'll just have to run for your late husband's seat in his stead, won't you?"

Cady met her enemy's eyes unflinchingly. She knew that Bruno had been furious when the governor had appointed her interim senator a few weeks after Rafe's accident. It had been Rafe's own wish, expressed through blinks when the state's chief executive had visited him in the hospital shortly before Rafe's transfer to the nursing home. What a blow to Bruno, who'd had Emmett lobbying in Albany for Bruno's appointment to the position. The governor had told her of Emmett and Bruno's machinations, and also of Rafe's insistence that Cady herself fill the office. For brief moments she had taken heart and embraced this trust as evidence that Rafe still loved her, despite their growing estrangement.

After all, she was only thirty, the minimum age required by the Constitution to serve as a U.S. senator, and despite having minored in political science in college, she had no previous experience in public office. So Rafe's desire that she fulfill his duties while he was unable to must be his way of expressing his love for her, she reassured herself momentarily.

But no, she told herself cynically after considering the matter, it was just that Rafe wanted to keep the Densmore name before the voters in the event that he recuperated sufficiently to resume his Senate seat and run for reelection. He knew that she would yield to him more readily than Bruno Trabold would. Ambition, not love, had dictated his actions.

"Cady? Cady, you're daydreaming again. Come back to me. All those troubles are behind you now. Dad and Bruno can't still be angry at you."

"That's what you think," Cady muttered, feeling her

insides flutter in pleasure when he laughed. Every sound he made was like a pearl to her after those long months of silence. "I've hired Albert Trock to take care of you and help you with the therapy program that you'll begin soon."

"I like him, Cady." Rafe grinned at her. "Although here in the hospital and in the nursing home, he didn't talk much more than I did. He's strong, though," Rafe mused. "He'd pick me up like the sack of meal I was and toss me around as though I weighed nothing."

"Graf likes him, too." Cady took a deep breath. "That's why I decided to give him the job...that and the fact that your father had him fired from the nursing home."

Rafe grimaced, nodding. "Emmett does not tolerate the kind of deceit Trock perpetrated against him." He looked at Cady for long moments. "He would no doubt like to fire you as my wife."

Cady glanced down at her clenched hands, noting the whiteness of her knuckles. "I'm sure he would leave that to you." Her voice was as hoarse as Rafe's.

"I hope he isn't holding his breath." Rafe's voice had a mocking lilt that made her smile. "That's better. I was beginning to think you would never smile for me again."

Cady erupted, all the volcano of worry that had lain deep in her coming to the surface like lava. "Do you think it was easy watching you all those months? Seeing you lying there, knowing that you hated it, that you would rather have died than be that way? Do you think it's..." She gulped air as she jumped to her feet, pacing back and forth next to Rafe's bed. "Do you think it's easy to walk up and down a hospital corridor counting the marks on the wall, trying to calculate in your mind the hours it took to paint the hall, because if you didn't do that you would start screaming? Do you know what it's like when the doctor comes out to tell you whether your husband is alive or...or..." Cady wrung her hands, her throat closing.

"Cady. Cady, come here," Rafe demanded, holding out his arms.

She went to him, her fist pressed to her mouth. "Oh, Rafe, Rafe, forgive me. I know you went through hell. I don't know what made me say those things."

Rafe pulled her down to the bed, cradling her in his arms. "Cady, thank you. Thank you for giving me back my life."

Cady took long, shuddering breaths, never wanting to move out of his arms, never wanting to be away from him. "Isn't it wonderful, Rafe? You're alive," she mumbled into his shoulder. "Really, really *alive*. They don't even have to monitor you with all those awful needles anymore."

Rafe nodded, his face pressed into her hair.

They started simultaneously at the sound of the door opening. "We should set up a schedule for visiting," Emmett growled, glaring at Cady.

"That wouldn't work, Father. I want Cady with me all the time, so the rest of the family can work around that."

Emmett looked from one to the other, Bruno at his back. "Well, don't expect me—or Bruno—to be grateful to your wife for keeping us in the dark. *We didn't like it.*" Her father-in-law gave Cady a heavy-browed look.

Rafe shrugged but didn't release Cady's hand.

In succeeding days, as Rafe continued to improve, the hospital was very understanding about Cady visiting at odd hours. The wing where Rafe's room was located was set apart, with an entrance of its own. After Cady obtained permission to use that entrance, she was at the hospital almost all the time.

Many nights she would just sit there and look at him, knowing that when he woke he would speak and move, talk and laugh. In these quiet moments when she could look at him, all she wanted was not to worry that someone could see the love she knew was spilling from her eyes. She loved Rafe with an unquenchable love, a love that had been alive from the time she met him and had not dimmed even in their estrangement. During his illness it had burned to an even greater intensity, so that Cady knew she would have no life without Rafe, that he was inside her, that he was her essence.

Sometimes while she waited for him to awaken, she would recite out loud all the business in the Senate that day. "Bailey's environmental bill is getting more support..." she would say.

Every time Cady looked at him, whether Rafe was awake or asleep, she could visualize the vital man he had been before the accident. Her pulse quickened at the thought of that six-foot-two-inch frame moving and laughing again. Those football shoulders, which should have looked incongruous in a silk suit, seemed sexy instead because his narrow hips and powerful thighs had such a masculine, virile appeal. Rafe had his mother's black Irish coloring. The other Densmore offspring had Emmett's sandy coloring. Rafe's dark brown hair had a persistent wave to it, including the wavy lock that fell forward on his forehead, making Cady's fingers itch to run through it. His strong, muscular body was belied by his supple hands with long, tapering fingers. Cady had often joked with him in the early days of their marriage that with such hands he should have been a pianist.

When she said that on their honeymoon, Rafe had gone to the piano in the lounge and sat down and played a love song, singing to her in a sure baritone that he loved her. If only he had meant those lyrics!

Yet with all his accomplishments, Cady could remember how Rafe had laughed when she told him that it was his strong-hewn face she loved, the sharp-drawn cheekbones that were almost Slavic in width, the wide-apart blue eyes with the girlishly thick lashes, the hard mouth with the soft lower lip whose fullness was a clue to the sensual man that Rafe was.

The family seemed to come out of the woodwork when word of Rafe's recovery hit the news. And hit the news it did. Even the wire services covered it. Rafe insisted that Cady read the story to him, since, as he explained, she had always read the news to him each day. She still visited him at the same time she had when he was in the nursing home, but now more often than not she would run into some other member of the family. She relaxed in the twins' company because they so obviously loved Rafe and were happy with the outcome of the operation.

"Even though you should have let us in on the scam, Cady," Gareth said reproachfully. "It would have been great to tweak Bruno Trabold's tail. The old man puts too much confidence in him, if you ask me."

Gavin, the quiet one, nodded once emphatically.

One afternoon, when Cady had had a particularly tough day at the Senate and was telling Rafe how pompous she thought a thirty-year member of that august body was, Rafe's two sisters swept through the door, looking every inch the wealthy Maryland society ladies they were.

"My dear Rafe," Aileen cried, bestowing a vague smile on Cady. "I just talked to our dear friend Hugo Billings, you know who I mean, don't you? He was at Harvard with Dave, a terribly successful surgeon. *He* says that the operation I described to him is very revolutionary and not positively safe." She turned her gaze full on Cady. "I can understand poor Daddy's reservations." She blinked. "It was a bit high-handed and thoughtless of you, Cady."

"High-handed and thoughtless," Aveen parroted, pushing aside the reading material that Cady had just brought Rafe and putting in its place a bouquet of flowers in a Wedgwood vase.

"I'm delighted that you're so glad to have me back among the living," Rafe pronounced, his dry tone not all due to his still-hoarse throat.

Aileen looked at him down her long, aristocratic nose. "Your welfare is not the issue here, Rafe, dear."

"Yes, Rafe, don't cloud the issue by talking about your health, dear." Aveen's smile was indulgent. "You don't want to be thought a hypochondriac. Very tacky."

"I'll try not to be tacky," Rafe assured his sisters ironically.

"Good," Aileen said, frowning as if already having

forgotten who she was censuring and why.

"He always took discipline well," Aveen assured her sister. She turned to Cady, a pained look on her face. "Cady, dear, I do so wish you wouldn't sit around with your mouth open. So déclassé, don't you see?" The lines between her eyes deepened. "I'm surprised that Rafe hasn't said anything to you about it." She pursed her lips at her brother. "I'm sure people know that Cady's related to us. You should say something."

"Cady, make a note that I'm to tell you that you mustn't sit around with your mouth open, no matter what my sisters say." Rafe smiled at his sisters in a bland way, ignoring their suspicious stares. Neither Aileen nor Aveen was known for having a sense of humor.

When her sisters-in-law left, Cady gave a huge sigh, not wanting to look at Rafe for fear she would laugh. But when she heard him chuckling, she let her own smile loose.

"Lord, they're incredible. Cady, you have my permission to shoot me if I ever get as pompous as my sisters." Rafe's blue eyes shone merrily into hers.

Cady giggled, loving the feeling of intimacy they were sharing. "I won't ask your permission. I'll just do it."

They laughed together. Then, as Cady watched, Rafe's smile seemed to harden. "Lying trapped in a tilted bed, I learned more about my own family than I ever did when we all occupied the same house. Lord, Cady, have they always acted toward you as if you're totally brainless? Don't they know about the great job you've done in the Senate?" His lips tightened even more. "Was I so damn blind that I didn't see the cavalier way they treated you? Damn it, Cady, why didn't you tell me I was a bigger ass than either of my sisters?"

Cady felt lighthearted and would willingly have let Rafe's sisters have another go at her without flying at them if it made Rafe so tender. She chuckled again.

"Share the joke."

"I was just thinking how much I've changed. When we first got married, I was so in awe of your sisters.

They were so tall, so imposing, so much the women in command. Now . . ." She shrugged.

"Now what, Cady?"

"Sometimes I'm afraid I'll laugh in their faces."

"Only sometimes?" Rafe flashed her the impish look that Cady loved so much, had so missed seeing.

She laughed, feeling weightless, treasuring these close moments with Rafe, moments that she hadn't shared with him in a long time, moments that had marked the early days of their marriage. Hope snowballed inside her that he wouldn't want to divorce her, that he might suggest they try again.

They were still laughing together when Bruno entered the room. "Your father is attending the rally for Congressman Sykes, but he wanted me to bring these figures that the Greeley people compiled on the nuclear power plant." Bruno barely nodded to Cady as he leaned over the end of the bed to hand Rafe a manila folder.

"Another plan on how to rape the planet, Bruno?" Cady queried, her voice mild, her pulse jumping when Rafe chuckled.

Bruno looked at her, his polar ice cap smile making her shiver. "No. Another plan to make the country richer."

"The country?" Cady scoffed. "Or a few vested interests whose under-the-table boss happens to be Mr. Greeley?"

"You're beginning to talk like Congressman Ardmore, that left-wing buddy of yours, Cady." The frigid display of teeth widened, reminding Cady of a shark. No one could call that a smile. Cady shuddered to herself.

"What are you saying, Bruno?" Rafe demanded, his voice expressionless.

"Nothing." He pulled a package of cigarettes from his pocket, then frowned at the No Smoking sign and returned them to his pocket. "We all thought Cady was having all those meetings with Rob Ardmore because they were both interested in archaeology." His glance slid off Cady's face, taking note of the two coin-size spots of color she felt burning in each cheek. "I can see now that they had more to . . . discuss than that. No wonder you met him so often, Cady."

He left, a satisfied look on his face.

Cady could feel the change. The closeness was gone. There was a chill in the air instead of laughter.

The balloon of hope burst palpably when she turned to look at her white-faced husband, his eyes leaping in cobalt fury.

2

RAFE STAYED IN the hospital longer than anticipated because he had to be introduced to his recuperation program under the aegis of his physical therapists and his doctors. Often after these sessions Rafe would be exhausted, and upon returning to his room he fell into a deep sleep.

It seemed to Cady that relations between them grew increasingly strained. She had tried to talk to Rafe about Rob Ardmore and how grateful she was to him for helping her through two rough periods, her adjustment to Rafe's debility and her work in the Senate. She couldn't bring herself to tell Rafe how lonely she had been, before and after his accident, how she had needed both a friend and a diversion to keep her sane. She had begun her studies in archaeology at Rob's instigation after they had talked one day about their majors in college.

"With your scientific background, Cady, I'll bet you'd enjoy these classes I'm auditing. Why don't you come with me one evening?" Rob had urged her.

To Cady, the classes had become a lifeline. It seemed

to her it was at that point that she had really begun to take hold of her life.

She shook herself out of her reverie and glanced at her slumbering husband. How boyish he looked in sleep! All the pain lines smoothed away, all the anger at Cady softened out of that firm mouth.

She sighed, trying to implant the image of that face on her mind against the time when she might be separated from him. "You've never known how much I love you, have you, Rafe? To you, I was just a star-struck schoolgirl you happened to marry. Oh, Rafe, don't you know that I willingly settled for anything you could give me, not because I was a silly college girl, but because even then, twelve years ago, at the age of eighteen, I loved you." She could feel her body tighten as though because she was saying the words, even in a whisper, she had to protect herself against Rafe's derision. "Not that you ever made overt fun of me, love. You didn't. But it always seemed as though you would reach a point where you would regret that I was your wife. It seems from the moment we married, I've been trying to harden myself against the day you would want to be free of me." She could feel her lips twist at the sound of her words. "Feeling sorry for yourself, Cady Densmore?" she quizzed herself. "No!" Cady almost shouted. Then she looked at the somnolent Rafe, afraid she might have wakened him. No, his lips were still parted in low snoring as sleep held him in its grip.

Her critical gaze took note that he seemed to have gained weight despite the arduous and often painful therapy sessions. Rafe was a fighter, too. They were both fighters. She had always known it about Rafe. She had only found it out about herself after Rafe's accident.

"I wasn't a fighter when you first met me, was I, Rafe? Otherwise I would have gone back to the dorm and punched Todd and Marina in the eye that day instead of running home and crying alone in my room. But then if I hadn't done that, maybe you wouldn't have met me. Just maybe if I hadn't kept you talking so long, you wouldn't have stayed at our house overnight." Cady yawned, her long day in the Senate office beginning to have its effect on her. She didn't want to sleep when she only had a short stay with Rafe. Perhaps if she just closed her eyes for a minute, she would be fresh and alert when he woke up.

As she fell into a half-doze, the memory came coursing back.

She was Cathleen Dyan Nesbitt, and she was eighteen and already a sophomore at Cornell, and she was in love with Todd Leacock, a twenty-year-old junior. At least that was what she thought was between them, until she had hotfooted it to her best friend's dorm room and found Todd in bed with Marina. He had laughed at her and told her to grow up, that shocked little virgins were out of style.

She had left the dorm and stumbled across campus and down the hill to the house she shared with her father, a professor of political science. She had heard him laughing with someone in the study, but she had gone right to her room to lie across the bed, wide-eyed, staring at the ceiling. "You won't die from this, Cady," she had muttered to herself. "It just feels like you're dying." She'd flopped over on her stomach and moaned into her pillow. She hadn't heard the bedroom door open.

"Your father thought you were home, and since his housekeeper is at the store, he told me to come and fetch you." The baritone voice had a sandpaper quality to it, making Cady assume that the speaker was a smoker. "Shall I tell him that you'd like to stay in your room for a while?"

Cady turned over and pushed herself to a sitting position on the bed. She started to say yes, she would prefer to remain in her room until dinner, when her eyes filled with tears once again, blinding her. She sat there seeing only the blurred outline of the man, not able to stanch the flow of her tears or articulate a word. She knew he was next to her when she felt the bed sag beneath his weight. He was a big man, and without thinking she moved to make more room for him.

"Don't cry. It can't be that bad. Did you get a bad grade? That happened to me, too, many times, but I survived. So will you." The coarse silk voice was comforting to Cady.

She had no idea how it happened, but all at once she was held against a worsted suit that had the softness of silk, the faint aroma of woodsy aftershave in her nostrils. "It wasn't my grades." She sobbed a sigh. "It was my boyfriend, Todd. I thought he loved me. He said he did." She lifted her head. "No wonder he wanted me to sleep with him. He wanted another scalp on his totem pole. If not mine, he'd take my best friend's." She glared at the man looking down at her, her eyes like wet amethysts.

"You found him with another woman." His hand pressed her head down again, stroking her honey-color hair that looked streaky blond in the summer. It was as thick and straight as rope.

"In bed with Marina," she gritted into the custom-tailored jacket. The stranger let his breath out in a long sigh. She felt it under her cheek. "Men do that sometimes. So do women. It's the chance you take in a relationship." He leaned back from her. "All the men who come into your life won't be like that."

"Would you be like that?" Cady snuffled, taking the fine linen handkerchief he offered her and blowing into it. "I'll wash this and send it to you," she muttered, pushing the hankie up the sleeve of her sweater.

"Thank you, but there's no need. You can keep it." He smiled at her and she almost gasped at the thickness of his lashes and the deep sky blue of his eyes.

"You didn't answer my question." She tried to sit straighter but was impeded by his body.

"No, I didn't. I wanted to ignore it, because I don't know the answer."

At this part of the memory Cady always squirmed, knowing that Rafe had given her a warning right then and there that she had not heeded. So what right had she now to resent the parties he went to without her?

"I think I would be faithful to a woman I loved and respected, but I don't know." He gave her a lopsided smile, his long finger touching her nose. "If I had someone like you, I don't think I'd want to risk losing her, but I'm also old enough to have had varied experiences with women and to want more." One dark brow rose as he studied her. "Have I shocked you, angel?"

"No. How old are you?"

"Twenty-nine."

Cady nodded. "And what do you do for a living? I suppose at one time you were here at the university and Father taught you?"

"Right. Then I went into the service for a while. When I came out I went to law school in Washington, and now I'm a congressman from downstate."

"Oh. Do you like it?"

"Very much. In fact, I'm thinking of running for the Senate next year."

"Really? Then I'll help you campaign." Cady wiped some moisture from her lashes. "I'd like that. And my minor is political science, my father's field, so perhaps I could be an asset to your campaign."

"Maybe you could help me find a wife first. My advisers tell me a wife is a great asset."

Cady laughed at his expression. "All right, I can do that for you."

"Be my wife, you mean." Rafe leaned toward her, one lazy finger running down her cheek.

Cady felt as though someone had pan-fried her skin. She tried to be as cool as he was. "Sure, if that's what you want. I can be terribly ladylike at times." She tried to hold his gaze, but her breathing was becoming constricted, so she looked away.

"I'll tell you what we'll do. Let's have dinner together with your father, then we'll take a walk and talk some more. But let's wait a bit before we join your father. I'd like to get to know you better, lady."

They had talked for a long time, skipping from topic to topic with the ease of long-time friends.

Not only had Cady never had the inclination to have men friends in her room, she was also sure that her solicitous father would not have approved. Yet she and Rafe sat on her bed and chatted in the most relaxed way, and she had felt no discomfort at all.

Finally, after she had laughed over a story he had told about his own clumsiness when he was first a congressman, Rafe leaned over and took her hand. "We've been up here quite a while, and I'm sure your father is wondering what's keeping me." He grinned at her. "You're easy to talk to, lady."

"Thank you." Cady grinned back, feeling a strange surge of power all at once.

Rafe looked down at the small hand almost lost in his long, graceful fingers. Then he looked up at her, his smile fading. "Your fall break is coming up, isn't it? Perhaps you and your father would like to join me at my place on Santo Tomas Island. I have a house there where I intended to unwind after the election. Do you think you would like to spend your vacation there?"

"Yes," Cady had answered promptly, then took his hand, rose from the bed, and accompanied him downstairs.

Dinner had been fun. She hadn't expected Rafe to be so knowledgeable of campus goings-on, but every time she told him about some antics she and her friends had participated in, he would relate some even more outrageous deeds that he and his friends had tried. Even her absentminded father was soon laughing.

They had walked after dinner and had not returned to the house until midnight. Cady felt as though she had known Congressman Rafe Densmore forever.

In the darkened living room of the old house, Cady had reached for the light switch.

"No, don't turn it on. There's enough light from the dying fire," Rafe had whispered, then he had pulled her down onto his lap. "You're fragile and too young," Rafe had whispered into her neck. "I don't know what's the matter with me." He muttered as though he were speaking to himself, but still he didn't release her. His hands were wandering seductively, caressing her neck, her shoulders, her breasts. "Does Todd touch you like this?" he said against her mouth as he pushed her back into the cushions.

"Sometimes." Cady gasped, not telling him that Todd had never made her body feel as though it were splintering into white-hot shards.

"Don't let him." Rafe's hands tightened on her. "I'm leaving early, before you get up, Cady, and if you're smart you'll tell me to go to my room now." His hands pushed under her sweater. "God, you should wear a bra...but I'm glad you don't." When he pushed the sweater up further and his mouth took hold of her nipple, Cady cried out, her body leaping in response to his.

"Easy, darling," Rafe had croaked. "I'm losing control."

"I don't care," Cady had moaned, her hands clutching him, wanting to belong to him.

"Cady." Rafe's mouth crashed into hers. His hands soothed her, aroused her, set her on fire.

When Rafe surged to his feet and set her away from him, Cady could only stand there open-mouthed as he tugged her sweater down in front, the slight tremor in his hands surprising her. "Get to bed right now," he said hoarsely. "I'll call you."

"Rafe," Cady had wailed.

"Now, Cady. Go to bed."

She had set her alarm so she would be up in time to see him, but he was already gone when she raced down the stairs at six o'clock the next morning.

"There's a crucial vote in the House today," her father had informed her in his placid way as the housekeeper poured his coffee. "Rafe's a good man. He was a good student, too." Professor Nesbitt sipped his coffee. "Ahhh. That's good. Doesn't need to work so hard, either, but he does."

"Are the Densmores rich, Father?"

"Yes. Rafe's father is in banking. A very shrewd,

tough man is old Emmett Densmore. Runs his family as he does his business, with an iron hand. Rafe has two sisters and twin brothers. He's the oldest."

Cady didn't dare pump her father anymore about Rafe. He was absentminded, but he was quite bright at reading people, and she didn't want him to see the effect that the downstate congressman had had on his daughter.

After the first week without a telephone call, Cady realized that Rafe wasn't going to phone. She fought despondency, throwing herself into the lab work and classwork that would let her forget sky-blue eyes and dark brown hair.

One afternoon, head down, hair whipping across her face, she headed across the quad, gold and russet maple leaves drifting to the ground, when suddenly someone took her arm. She squinted sideways to see who it was and nearly dropped her books.

"Hello, Cady." Rafe reached for the teetering books and slipped them under one arm, taking hold of her with the other. "Can we still get a cup of coffee in here?" he asked, pushing open the door of the Student Union.

The laughter, shouts, and clanking dishes faded to quiet for Cady as Rafe sat in front of her, a cup cradled in his hands. "What are you doing here?" she asked. She took too big a swallow of the coffee and coughed.

"Have you missed me?" He gave her a lopsided grin. "I missed you. I can only stay a few minutes; then I have to get back to my constituency." He shot out his wrist, looking at his gold wristwatch. "I have a plane standing by." He looked at her again, taking hold of one of her slender hands. "Tiny lady, I've missed you. I've arranged to have you and your father come down to Santo Tomas with me the day after the election." His smile turned her heart over. "So you see, you'll either have to commiserate with me or celebrate with me."

"I know you'll win." She had been breathless when he had squeezed her shoulders while he helped her on with the down vest she was wearing as they were leaving.

Several people spoke to her, and she responded, but she could never have said who they were a few moments later.

Rafe sheltered her with his arm when they were on the quad again and the wind whistled around them. She saw the Mercedes with a chauffeur behind the wheel parked near the stone wall. She looked up at Rafe, one eyebrow raised.

"A rented car," he answered her look before assisting her into the car and giving the chauffeur the directions to her house. When he enfolded her in his arms and began kissing her, she had no defense. Her parted lips welcomed his searching tongue as though she had been waiting for it all her life. "Lord, Cady, have you been practicing?" Rafe's voice was hoarse.

She shook her head, reveling in the feel of the crisp, dark hair at the nape of his neck. "It just comes natural with you." She giggled.

"Make sure it's just me," he muttered into her mouth as one hand loosened her jacket and felt for her breast. "Damn this election for keeping me from you." The car stopped and he looked at her long and hard. "I won't see you before we leave for Santo Tomas Island. Don't forget me."

She shook her head as he helped her from the car, gave her a hard kiss, and then sped off down the street. She was still shaking her head when she walked up the sidewalk and into her house.

That night Todd called her. "How about a beer at the Union?" Cady didn't hesitate. "I'm busy." She had no desire even to talk to Todd, much less meet him for a beer.

"Busy with that old man I saw you with in the Union this afternoon?" Todd sneered.

"Drop dead." Cady slammed down the phone.

Rafe had won, not by a landslide but still by a big margin. The trip to New York was throat-choking because she knew that Rafe would meet them there. It had been a wrenching disappointment when they received the message that Rafe would join them on Santo Tomas a little later and that they were to go ahead.

Her first day on Santo Tomas Island was like a first day in paradise. The sand was white, the sea was blue. It was a private island, and Rafe's bungalow seemed to be the only one.

She swam while her father read, but she was just marking time until Rafe came.

By the time he arrived the next day, Cady had begun to feel uncomfortable and was wishing that she hadn't come. Her father had been content as soon as he found the well-stocked library.

At first Cady wouldn't look at Rafe when he arrived. He had another man with him, Bruno Trabold, whom he described as a special assistant to his father. "And he's been invaluable to me in this election." Rafe had slapped the man on the back and grinned at him companionably. He hadn't seemed to notice Bruno's hot-eyed assessment of Cady in her pink bikini. She had felt very uncomfortable.

Rafe had taken her by the hand and pulled her up the stairs to his bedroom, calling to Bruno to introduce himself to Professor Nesbitt in the library.

"Before your suspicious little soul rebels at being up here, let me tell you that I have every intention of changing and showering in my bathroom while you remain here." He wrapped her in his arms as soon as he closed the bedroom door. "But I want to feel you close to me," he mumbled into her hair. "I've missed you, angel."

"Congratulations," Cady squeaked, feeling all her uncomfortable sensations at his tardiness fading away, wanting him to continue to stroke her breast. "I like being up here with you. I miss you, too."

Rafe lifted her onto his bed, then stretched out beside her. "It feels very right, having you here like this," his voice rasped against her cheek, before his mouth nibbled its way to hers. "Kiss me, Cady."

Her mouth flowered open under his, her hands straining her to him. Her body made restless motions under his as his hands pushed at the scraps of cloth covering her.

All at once he rolled over and sat upon the bed, taking deep gulps of air. "I have to take a shower. Don't move."

"Rafe." Feeling languid, Cady lifted her arms.

"No." He strode toward the bathroom, only looking back when he stood in the doorway. "Just wait there for me, Cady. I won't be ten minutes. I have something I want to ask you and I won't be able to concentrate very well as it is." His smile was a derisive twist of his mouth, but his eyes were hot as they roved over her body.

"That had to be the fastest shower on record." Cady giggled at him as he strode across the bedroom toward her, just a few minutes later, dressed casually in light slacks and a knit shirt, toweling his hair.

He tossed the towel in a careless heap on the floor, then sat down beside her, his thigh touching hers. He put a hand to her hair, threading his fingers through it. "You have lovely hair. The sun shines in it." He nuzzled her cheek with his nose. "I was afraid you might go downstairs again if I didn't hurry, and I have something to say to you."

Cady's heart was thudding wildly. Her eyes were so close to Rafe's indigo gaze that she could see the tiny gold streaks that rayed out in his irises. "What . . . what is it?" she choked.

"Marry me." His mouth closed over hers, his tongue intruding into her mouth to tease and coax her tongue. "Marry me, angel. I want you." He leaned over her as he pushed her back onto the bed. "You're too young, I know that, but I can't wait for you. I want you now."

Cady pulled him down to her, her body feverish. She prayed she wasn't dreaming. She had thought of their first conversation so many times, she felt she might be dreaming now. He had been kidding before when he had sat on her bed and asked her to be his wife. Was he kidding her now? "Do you mean it?" she asked.

Rafe pulled back from her, the bones of his face seeming to push through the skin, his mouth a hard slash
across it. "Oh, yes, I mean it. Am I too old for you?"

"Oh, Rafe, you're perfect for me. I love you, Rafe."
Cady's fingers dug into his neck, urging him down to
her.

He didn't relent for a moment but gave her a long
look, his eyes like cobalt rays. "Someday you may change
your mind, Cady. You're so young to be subjected to
the pressures of being a politician's wife. I know damn
well you should be going to fraternity dances and beer
blasts, but I can't let you go. I only hope you don't hate
me for this later and decide to leave me."

"I won't ever want to leave you. Aren't you going to
kiss me?" She laughed up at him, feeling eleven feet tall
and able to leap skyscrapers in a single bound.

His mouth was gentle on hers at first; then, as she
wriggled under him, the kiss deepened, his hands trembling as they explored her, touching every pore.

Cady could feel the bowstring tension of his body as
he tried to keep himself in check. She had no such in-
hibitions with him, letting her restless limbs telegraph
the need she had for him. With a sense of power she
could feel him slipping toward her, his iron control melting as their bodies strained toward one another through
their clothing.

"Hey, Rafe, are you in there? I think the professor is
getting worried about his daughter."

Rafe looked down at her, his eyes blinking as he tried
to surface from the whirlpool of desire into which both
of them had been drawn. "All right, Bruno. We're coming." Rafe took a deep breath and then looked down at
her again, one hand pushing back the dampened tendrils
of hair at her temples. "Saved by the knock on the door,"
he said lightly. "It's a good thing Bruno came when he
did. I think I would have taken you right here."

"I think Bruno is a busybody and I wish he would

mind his own business," Cady hissed, her fingers running down his nose.

Rafe laughed and reached for her hand, letting his tongue trail down the lifeline of her palm. "Let's go down and tell your father that we don't want a long engagement. I don't think I could take it."

"Neither could I," Cady murmured as Rafe set her on her feet, then tightened the ties of her bikini.

"Do you have a beach jacket you could wear over that?" He led her out into the hall. "I don't think I would like even your father looking at you in that pink bikini."

Cady's laugh trilled down the hall as she delighted in the possessive gleam in his eye. Before they went to her father in the library, Cady fetched a beach jacket in pink terry cloth.

"I'm not totally satisfied, because those long legs are delicious and they are showing, but it's better than before." Rafe kissed her lingeringly.

At once Cady stepped closer and wrapped her arms about his neck, her tongue thrusting at his.

"Cady, angel, don't," Rafe groaned, pushing back from her and holding her arms at her sides. "I'll be dragging you back up the stairs in a minute." He threaded his fingers through hers and pushed open the door of the library, where Bruno was handing Cady's father a drink. "Would you mind leaving us alone for a few minutes, Bruno?" Rafe smiled at the man, then turned to the professor.

Cady felt a frisson of trepidation race down her spine when she looked at Bruno. Then the flicker that she saw in his eyes as he looked at Rafe was gone. It was easy for her to blame her imagination. The golden aura she floated in didn't allow for anyone's disaffection.

"Ah—Professor Nesbitt . . . ah, sir, could I speak with you a moment?" Rafe tightened his grip on Cady's hand as her father pushed his glasses back onto his head and looked at their clasped hands with a narrowed gaze. "I've asked Cady to marry me, sir, and she's said yes. I'd like you to give us your blessing." Rafe had sounded very formal to Cady.

Her father rose to his feet. "Cady?" He looked at her long and hard.

She freed herself from Rafe's grip and went to embrace her father. "I love Rafe and want to marry him. Please say you're happy for me."

"And what of your studies at the university?" Her father stroked her head pressed to his chest.

"I've thought of that, sir," Rafe said, coughing. "She could continue her studies at Georgetown or George Washington University or any of the many schools in Washington. She only has two years..." Rafe's voice trailed off. Cady could see the deep red color staining Rafe's neck as he looked at her father.

"Ahem." Professor Nesbitt looked at Rafe, his face not unfriendly, but not totally open, either. "I see that you've given this much thought."

"I've had a hard time thinking of anything but Cady since I met her." Rafe's laugh was brittle.

"But you kept enough of yourself apart to concentrate on the election," her father mused, sighing as he looked at Cady's moonstruck face.

"I had to concentrate on the election, yes." Rafe watched Professor Nesbitt, his eyes wary.

"Please, Father, I want to marry him. I can't be happy without Rafe," Cady pleaded, only taking passing notice of the rather sad look on her father's face.

"Yes, I can see that you're in love, child." Professor Nesbitt embraced his daughter. "I want you to be happy."

Their wedding was supposed to be a small one. Both Rafe and Cady had agreed on a ceremony in the Cornell Chapel and a small dinner party afterward with just a few family members.

Emmett Densmore had tried to change that, insisting that the wedding be held in St. Patrick's Cathedral in New York City. When Cady balked, her father intervened and told Emmett that the wedding would take place in the chapel. Rafe sided with the professor.

Cady mumbled in her sleep, still seeing in her mind's eyes the fomenting rage in the elder Densmore when he was thwarted on the wedding plans and remembering with horror the circus of people at the reception, people Emmett had insisted on inviting.

"Don't worry, darling, we'll be leaving soon and won't have to bother with any of them," Rafe had whispered into her ear, his hand caressing her spine.

"But how about poor Father?" she had said, sipping from the champagne glass that Rafe held to her lips.

"If I know my new father-in-law, he'll just quietly disappear after a suitable time and go home." Rafe laughed, leading her out onto the dance floor of the country club that Emmett Densmore had rented for the day; he had herded the guests there after the small dinner party hosted by her father for the small number of people who had been invited to the wedding.

Cady had been aghast at the large group assembled at the country club and had been glad of Rafe's constant presence at her side. He hadn't faltered once when he introduced her to their guests in the long and tedious receiving line that Emmett had insisted on.

"Damn it, boy, you have to keep the image intact. You're a politician." He had looked at Cady, a hint of contempt in his smile. "I assume that your schoolgirl bride understands what a politician is. A woman like Lee Terris would have had no trouble in understanding. You dated her for a long time."

Rafe had stiffened at Cady's side, his arm pulling her even closer to him. "Cady understands my life and will be an active part of it." His voice lowered. "I won't let anyone put her down—not anyone, do you hear me?"

Father looked at son, their wills concrete walls pushing against each other.

"You don't have to protect your wife from Densmores, boy. She's one herself now." Emmett's voice was hearty, but his eyes were as hard and cold as slate.

Their honeymoon had been paradise. The first evening, when Bruno Trabold called, Rafe had told him not to call again, that he was unhooking the phone and that they would be back from Santo Tomas Island in three weeks.

They had sipped more champagne, and between sips Rafe had kissed her. "I feel I've waited forever for you, Cady, love." He had loosened her hair from the fashionable chignon that Cady was sure made her look more sophisticated. "I don't like all that sunlight twisted and tied back." He had eased the blouse from her shoulders. "God, Cady, of all days for you to wear a bra," Rafe had groaned.

She had laughed, feeling excited but not the least worried. She was where she belonged, in the arms of the man she loved and who loved her. Her fingers began an exploration of their own, unbuttoning his shirt and tangling themselves in the hair on his chest. When she felt his chest contract, her pulse quickened.

"Cady, darling, I'm going to kiss every inch of your body," he growled into her neck, his hands busy at her skirt zipper. "You're not frightened, are you, angel?"

"No. I'm where I want to be." Cady nuzzled her lips along his jawline, liking the fresh-shaven feel.

"I hope you won't mind spending three weeks in bed," Rafe muttered, his lips pulling on one nipple until it was like a pale ruby. His left hand cupped the fullness of the other breast, his thumb gently stroking the nipple.

"How did you get my clothes off so fast?" Cady asked with a dazed gasp.

"I've been practicing in my dreams since I met you," Rafe rumbled, not moving his face from between her breasts as his hands continued down her body, now naked to his eager ministrations. "Undress me, love."

Cady's hands had never been faster or surer as she helped him disrobe. She wanted to be close to Rafe, to belong to him. Nothing and no one would ever separate them then. She felt the cushions of the couch shift as he levered himself erect with her in his arms. "I never knew that a man could have such a beautiful body," she crooned, her index finger curving down his ear to his neck.

Rafe's laugh was hoarse as he mounted the stairs two at a time. "I'm glad you like my body, angel, because I love yours." His mouth closed over hers in a hard kiss. "I wanted to make love to you the first time up here where we almost made love before, the day we became engaged."

"The day Bruno interrupted us. I remember." Cady frowned.

"Don't think of anyone but me now, wife," Rafe commanded as he followed her down to the bed, his hands and mouth taking possession of her at once. "I want you to stay with me always, Cady," Rafe had moaned to her as Cady feather-touched his spine.

"I'll never go unless you send me away." Her voice had faded as sensations erupted like a flash flood, her hands coming up to clutch him, her body turning to molten lava.

When he lifted himself over her, Cady was eager for him. The sudden pain came as a surprise. Before it could register, Rafe was soothing her, beginning a rhythm that started her spinning. She heard someone calling Rafe's name, and through a hot pink haze she realized it was herself.

"Darling, I can't hold back any longer," Rafe had called to her, but Cady hadn't heard him. The vortex had caught her as well and spun them together off the planet.

Cady felt as though her body had been oiled from the inside out as she relaxed against Rafe, their bodies sliding together.

It had been like that for three weeks. They had made love wherever they happened to be at the time—the beach, the living room, the sea. It had been idyllic, a dream.

Where had the dream gone? What had happened to pull them apart? It wasn't just the snide innuendos of Bruno Trabold and Emmett, even though their attitude helped widen the fissure in their marriage. What had been the real weapon that corroded and eroded their relationship?

The nightmare questions shook her from her reverie. She looked into the blue-ice of her husband and felt afraid.

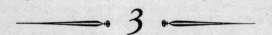

3

AFTER SEVERAL WEEKS of intensive speech and physical therapy, Rafe was pronounced fit enough to go home. His physical therapy would be continued with the male nurse Trock, who had come to work for Cady soon after Rafe's operation. Trock had told Cady he was willing to take instruction in the procedures that Rafe would be using and that he had a general knowledge of therapy from his many years working at nursing homes and previously at a veterans' hospital.

It would have been so perfect, Cady thought, if Rafe did not still have that coldness in his eyes whenever they were alone. To his credit, he treated her with warmth in the presence of others and was very supportive of her in front of his family.

Cady had made up her mind that if they were to get a divorce, the suggestion wouldn't come from her. She felt a simmering hurt that all her efforts to bring Rafe back to the land of the living might result in losing him. That painful smolder lasted about a week after Rafe came home. Then the pain turned to anger. To hell with it, Cady thought, I'm not walking a tightrope anymore. I won't give Rafe up without a fight, she ruminated to herself one day while she was out riding, but I damn well am not going to wear my heart on my sleeve.

She could see Rafe's puzzlement at her new, relaxed attitude. Her offhand way with him seemed to make him wary at first, then she sensed a sort of relieved air about him. He began to treat her much the same way. Cady still felt the estrangement between them, but there was an understanding now, a cautious acceptance of each other.

She felt relieved by the strong support Rafe gave her whenever his family was near. It was obvious to her that her father-in-law had not forgiven her for bypassing him and insisting that Rafe have the operation. Emmett Densmore had a long memory, and he would not forget that Cady had deceived him. Even though he was happy that his son was getting back to full strength, Emmett would not forget what Cady had done. Most of the time when Emmett visited, she avoided him.

One day, when Rafe had been out of the hospital for several weeks and was able to pull himself around with the help of two canes, Emmett arrived in his usual whirlwind manner, Bruno at his side.

Cady was out on the back lawn watching Trock lift Rafe into part of the complicated gym apparatus that had been installed both inside and outside the house. She wasn't quick enough to retreat. She had turned to see what had made Graf rise to his feet and growl. She sighed, wishing that Durra weren't just across the county into Maryland but across the country instead.

"Why don't you get rid of that dangerous dog, Cady?" Emmett snapped, looking with distaste from Cady to the brown Doberman. "He could be a danger to Rafe."

"He loves Rafe." Cady cleared her throat.

Emmett fixed her with a gimlet gaze. "And how would you know what's good for my son?" he hissed, his eyes sliding to Rafe some distance away, then back again.

"When have you ever known what was right for him? God knows, and so do I, that you're not the right wife for him. He needs a strong woman like Lee Terris, not a cream puff like you." Emmett spat out the words as though something had soured his taste buds.

Cady ignored Bruno's chuckle, feeling the blood drain downward in her body. "When Rafe was ill," she said, her voice expressionless though her insides were churning, "the dog provided needed diversion for him. Graf now has the idea that he must care for Rafe. He is never far from Rafe or Trock," she finished woodenly.

"And that's another thing." Emmett bit off the end of his cigar and allowed Bruno to light it for him. "That man Trock—what do you know about him? Why have you let him move in here? I don't trust him, and I can't forget how he kept me at that damned nursing home with a cock-and-bull story about Rafe having gone for some special kind of physical therapy while in reality my son was undergoing a dangerous operation without my consent. Of course you cooked up that story for him to tell me." His heavy-lidded gaze narrowed on her. "I won't forget that, Cady."

Cady forced herself not to shudder, keeping her eyes on Rafe's slow but steady approach across the lawn. He had dropped the canes and was making way under his own power.

Some feet away Rafe stopped to catch his breath, his eyes going from Cady to his father. "What are you saying to my wife, Dad?" His voice was almost at the deep timbre it had been before the accident. "I don't like that white face she gets when you're around her." His eyes had the fathomless expression they often wore when he looked at her.

Emmett bristled. "How do you expect me to feel toward her after she bamboozled me like that? You know what she did." With one more grim look at his daughter-in-law, Emmett strode toward his son, slapping him on the back. He ignored Trock and looked askance at the dog who ambled at Rafe's side.

"Yes, I know what Cady did for me. She saved my life. She did everything necessary to see that my wishes were honored." Rafe looked straight at Cady again. "I won't have her intimidated in any way," he warned, repeating what he had said on their wedding day.

"Don't be a fool, boy." As the dog crowded next to Rafe when he took a chair, Emmett glared. "Get rid of that dog. Have it destroyed. It's dangerous."

Rafe rubbed the silken, pointed ears, the strong brown neck. "I can't do that. He's a friend." Rafe smiled as the dog rubbed his strong muzzle against his master's hand. "Cady found him near our summer home on Lake Cayuga. Graf was a starving pup then." The Doberman wagged his minuscule tail as though he knew they were talking about him. "Now he looks more like a deer than a dog. A real beauty, isn't he?" He looked over at his father, who had just drawn up another lawn chair beside his son's. "You have something on your mind, Dad. What is it?"

"Now that you're easing back into the job and will soon begin a full-scale campaign, I want you to do something about that nuclear power plant on the Hudson that Greeley is so interested in..." Emmett began, flicking the ash from his cigar onto the flagstone patio.

"I'm sorry, Dad, but Cady has made me see what a destructive thing that would be for the environment. She's fully researched it, and I have no quarrel with her facts, so the answer is no."

"What?" Emmett surged to his feet, tossing his cigar down with a hard thrust, missing the Doberman by inches. "I told Greeley he could count on your support."

"Then tell him you were wrong. I was keeping an open mind about supporting the measure before the accident, but I hadn't had a chance to look into the specifics. Cady has. She's shown me the damage that it would do to wildlife and the existing fishing in the area, as well as the sordid profit motive of its promoters. I won't support it."

"You're going to listen to a half-baked girl who doesn't

know—" Emmett huffed, a dark red mottling his neck and cheeks.

"Cady is a thirty-year-old woman who has done a good job for the state of New York." Rafe's voice was granite hard, his eyes blue chips of anger.

"Are you going to turn your back on the political machine that elected you?" Emmett bellowed, bringing a wary Graf to his feet. "And you keep that damn dog off me or I'll bring a gun next time I come and shoot it myself. Come on, Bruno, let's get out of here before I really let go."

The two men had almost rounded the house when Rafe called to them. "Cady is having that barbecue on Saturday. I assume you're coming." His voice was mild.

"Yes, I am, damn you, if for nothing else than to make sure you don't let that scheming wife of yours sink your political boat altogether," Emmett fumed, turning away and charging toward the bright yellow Rolls-Royce where Bruno was holding the passenger-side door open.

"You should do twenty more of the hand pulls, Senator," Trock said woodenly, handing two metal grips to Rafe.

"We can pass for now, Trock," Rafe answered, handing the grips back to the attendant.

"Do it now," Trock insisted, his hand softly prodding Graf's neck.

"Don't argue," Cady said, laughing, as she urged Rafe back toward the outdoor gym. "You know he won't give up."

"Trock, when I'm strong enough, I'm going to chain you to that gym out there and leave you." Rafe glared at the other man.

"All right, Senator, do that. For now get back to work." The phlegmatic Trock waited until Rafe moved and then followed him.

Cady felt a glow as she watched Rafe pull himself up on the bars. He no longer needed his wheelchair, and like today, when his father was around, he sometimes eschewed the use of his twin metal canes.

She sighed when she thought of Saturday and the crowd that it would bring to the Highlands, their home in Virginia. She longed for the anonymity that their summer home in upstate New York always gave them. The people there weren't impressed with having a senator in residence, and Cady always felt a freedom in Ithaca that she could not find elsewhere.

"Cady?" Rafe gave a twist of a smile when she jumped. "I didn't mean to startle you. I just wanted to tell you that I know how hard it is for you to deal with my family and that I appreciate the way you try to get along with them." He licked his lips and smiled at Trock when the man handed him a frosted glass of lemonade. He took a long drink, looked at Cady, then away again. "I know it must have been hell for you all that time, working as hard as you did in my office, then coming to visit me every day . . . not missing once."

"Stop. Don't say any more, Rafe. I wanted to . . ." Cady began.

"I have to say it, Cady. If I live five lifetimes, I won't be able to thank you for what you did for me." He took a deep breath. "No matter how things go for us . . . I won't let anyone—and that includes my family—hurt you in any way if I can prevent it. You'll never have reason to be ashamed of me again as a husband." He tried to smile. "I'll do everything I can to ensure your happiness."

Cady stared at the red circles high on Rafe's cheekbones and wondered if he realized that she knew about the parties at Durra or the scandal that had been a political mini volcano at the time. She wondered if he was aware that Bruno Trabold had been most eager to keep her informed of the many call girls and political groupies who still went to Durra and elsewhere to enliven the good times of Rafe and his friends. Cady sighed inwardly. To give Rafe credit, since his release from the hospital, he hadn't attended any of these gatherings. He really wasn't strong enough to party, she thought. She swallowed, looked at her husband, and nodded.

* * *

On Saturday Rafe surprised her by saying that he would supervise the cooking of the special white hots, the pork frankfurters that were made only in Rochester, New York, and were a delight to everyone who tried them at their parties.

Cady had often heard the story about the German butchers who had emigrated to the upstate city and settled in sections that retained their unusual nicknames even after the city had grown up around them. She watched as her husband laid out the barbecuing equipment he would need.

"The first area is quite old," Rafe explained, a rueful smile on his lips as if acknowledging that he had told her all of this at some earlier time. "It was called the Butter Hole. The other section is called simply Dutchtown. The strong heritage of these people kept them making sausage in the old country way. Pork hots are the happy result of this."

"I love them myself," Cady confessed. "I let other people eat the beef barbecue, the ribs, and the chicken. I love the hots." She giggled. "Some of the people coming today won't be comfortable with any of the food we're serving. Should I have had side dishes of Beluga caviar?"

The shout of laughter from Rafe made her heart sing. He was getting well! She smothered the inner voice that reminded her that he might seek a divorce as soon as he was fully recovered. She wouldn't think of that now.

Cady felt a well of depression pull at her. Now was the time to explain about Rob Ardmore. Now was the time to assure Rafe that Rob was a friend, sometimes even a lifeline to her when she was trying to battle the frustrations of the Senate and the unyielding wall that Emmett and his cohorts had erected against her.

Then Trock was there handing her the barbecue aprons. The moment passed and she still hadn't said anything. She looked at Rafe as she gave one of the aprons to him, seeing the shuttered look come over his face again. What was he thinking? Could he read her mind? Did he know she was thinking of Rob Ardmore? Did he misunderstand her friendship with the Iowan representative? Perhaps Rafe was wondering what she knew about his private life before they met. Would he guess that she knew about Durra and the parties there? Was that why he had looked so flushed when he had talked to her moments before?

Lord, if she didn't stop this infernal soul searching, she would go crazy.

She turned to Trock and handed him the other apron, watching with intense concentration while he tied it around his waist, then walked back to bring the supplies to the two outdoor bars.

Rafe had still not put his on when he took a step that put him directly in front of her. "You seem to go into these blue funks often, Cady. It isn't too flattering for a man when he finds that his wife is preoccupied much of the time she's in his company." Rafe smiled, but the bones of his face seemed to be pushing through the flesh as he watched her.

"Cady? Cady, what are you dreaming about?" Rafe put one hand under her chin as they stood beside the twin ovens of the outdoor cooker with the huge grills on either side. "Were you thinking of your father?"

Cady smiled, neither confirming nor denying it, eyeing the first arrivals with a measure of relief.

"I know you miss the professor and want to go home." Rafe leaned down, just brushing his lips on hers. "When we talked to him on the phone on Wednesday, I told him we would be coming home as soon as the Senate adjourns."

Cady leaned back, her eyes widening. "We're not staying for those socials your father has arranged?" She felt her breath catch in her throat at the warm look in his eyes, then exhaled in an audible sigh of relief.

"No." He grinned. "I feel we can do more good back in our state, campaigning. My advisers tell me that we should hit the campaign trail early because the Harris poll shows that my opponent, this man Salters, is gaining on me." He stroked her jaw lightly. "Somehow I don't feel too worried. You did a very good job for me, Mrs. Densmore, and the feedback from the state echoes that. I don't know if I ever told you how much—"

Before he could finish, a sultry voice sent a shiver down Cady's spine. Before she could turn she knew that Lee Terris, the woman Emmett had wanted Rafe to marry, had arrived. Instead Lee had married the junior senator from Ohio just weeks after Cady and Rafe's wedding. Now divorced, she had resumed her maiden name—and predatory ways.

"Well, darling, are you going to ignore your guests?" Lee was ebony-haired and tall. In black slacks and shirt, she looked like a very shapely piece of black velvet from head to toe. Lee was a confident woman who had all the gloss that finishing school and money could provide. She moved toward Rafe and took hold of his arm, her long scarlet nails digging into his flesh as she reached up and kissed him.

Cady could feel her own fingernails digging into her palms. But instead of walking away, as she had done in the past when Lee had accosted Rafe similarly at other functions, she stood her ground, keeping her eyes on the couple and fighting to keep a bland look on her face.

When Rafe lifted his head, he reached out for Cady's hand. "I believe you know my wife, Lee. Cady, you remember Lee Terris?"

Cady nodded neutrally. "Yes, we've met. How are you, Lee?" When the divorcée made no response, continuing to grasp Rafe's arm proprietarily, Cady added demurely, "Would you mind moving back from Rafe just a bit? Heavy perfume makes him sneeze."

"Really?" Lee Terris gave Rafe a melting look. "He never used to mind my scent."

"Since his illness, his tastes have become more discriminating." Cady gave the other woman a wide smile, taking note of the angry intake of air. She turned to look up at Rafe. "Shall we greet the others? Trock will make the fires." She couldn't tell if there was a hint of amusement on Rafe's face as he inclined his head at her and excused himself from Lee Terris.

"I do believe your mouse just roared, Rafe darling," Lee cooed at their backs. "Perhaps she's planning on making her interim position in your office permanent."

Rafe urged her forward, but Cady balked, loosening herself very gently from his grip. "Ms. Terris, my husband is the senator from New York and that's how it is going to stay. We will campaign hard and he will win again. If there are any other questions you would like to ask me, please feel free." Cady didn't look at Rafe as she took his arm again, letting him lead her to a cluster of people that were moving from the house to the lawn.

The barbecue went well. It pleased Cady that so many of Rafe's friends in government came. She was surprised when many of these men and women came up to her and congratulated her on some work or another, or just came up to chat. It gave her a warm glow to see how easily they accepted her now. Before Rafe's accident, she had been too shy even to speak to many of them, but now, after her own small stint as Rafe's stand-in, she had a newborn confidence in her ability to tackle anything.

"I don't suppose we'll have any more of those luncheons," Rob Ardmore whispered behind her. "I really enjoyed them." He smiled at her as she turned to give him her hand.

"There won't be any need for me to be clued in on congressional strategies by the able congressman from Iowa." Cady laughed at him, glad that he had come. She considered Rob a good friend. More than once he had answered a question, dealt with a problem, and otherwise given her support. "It's good to see you, Rob. I feel as though I have one friend at this stampede."

He didn't release her hand at once. "I am your friend, Cady, and your admirer. No one could fault your devotion and care to a very ill man." He stared down at her from his medium height, his dark brown hair almost the same color as his eyes. "But Rafe is well now, and you have your own life to think of. You told me once that Rafe would have divorced you if he hadn't been in that plane crash." His hand tightened on hers. "No, don't look away. Cady, I never spoke to you while Rafe was convalescing. I didn't think that you could handle another crisis. But now he's well, and I want you to think of me as more than a friend."

"I should never have discussed Rafe with you," she reproached herself.

"Who else were you going to talk to? Emmett? Bruno Trabold? Hell, Cady, they would crucify you if they could. Your father was too far away. You needed me. I liked that, Cady. I need you now."

"Rob, I'm married. Rafe is still recuperating." Cady swallowed. "Besides, he hasn't mentioned anything about a divorce."

"Don't wait for him to mention it. Ask him for one, Cady," Rob urged, stepping closer to her.

She looked away from him, her head whirling. Her wandering eyes looked right into the blue steel of her husband's. "I have to go. I have guests, Rob." She pulled her hand free and walked at an angle toward the portable bar that had been set on a shady corner of the patio. She looked at the professional face of the hired barman and ordered a glass of mineral water and lime.

"Well, well, it looks as though the lovely ice maiden is branching out in all directions," Bruno Trabold offered, his voice as smooth as the smile he gave her. "First you take on the Senate so well that the word goes out that you could become a senator yourself. Now you seem to want to try a different man." He saluted her with his glass and leaned closer to her, his unbuttoned sport shirt opening to reveal the thick mat of hair on his muscular chest. "Let me offer myself as an alternative, Cady," he said, leering at her. "I have always found you most appealing, even if the Old Man doesn't."

"Thank you." Cady let her teeth show in the smile she gave him. She leaned forward and with one finger pulled the front of Bruno's shirt more open. She looked up to see the puzzled but not displeased look on his face, and she let her smile widen as she tipped the full glass of mineral water, ice, and lime into the shirt. "Have a good day, Bruno," she whispered over the loud yelp he gave. She turned at once and walked toward the other bar, set further out on the lawn under a dogwood tree. Again she ordered a drink. This time she sipped it with great relish.

"I saw that." Rafe placed his hand at her waist, smiling at a couple who waved to them. "What was it all about?"

Cady wasn't going to say anything, but the words rose out of her of their own volition. "That was Bruno offering himself to me as a worthy substitute. He seems to think I'm on the prowl."

"And are you?" Rafe rasped, the fingers at her waist clenching. "I watched Rob Ardmore with you. He's in love with you." He spat the words like hot rivets. "I once told you that I would let you go if you ever wanted out."

"So you did." Cady cleared her throat. "Perhaps we should see to our guests and save this talk for another time."

"Are you in love with him, Cady?" he snarled, his hand locking her to his side, the lean face, still pale from his long confinement, taking on a granite look.

Cady glanced up at him, all thought of responding in anger evaporating as she saw the fatigue bracketing his mouth and pinching at his eyes. "You're tired. It's been too much for you today." She slipped one arm around his waist. "Why don't you lie down for a little while and rest?"

"Will you come with me?" Rafe let his hand slide around her, then upward under her breast, his chin resting on her hair.

Cady didn't know what she was going to say until the words spilled from her mouth. "Yes, if you want me to, I'll go with you."

"Oh, I want you to, all right." Rafe gave a mirthless laugh.

"Damned impolite of you, Cady, to stand here and

let your guests shift for themselves," Emmett barked, distaste twisting his mouth as he looked at their entwined arms. "And Bruno says you were damned clumsy and spilled a drink down the front of his shirt. Now he's had to go and change. Damned inefficient, I'd say. It's about time you learned how important a political machine is, Cady, and got your priorities straight." Her father-in-law almost bit his cigar in half when Rafe only pulled her closer.

"You tell Bruno for me that if I catch him near my wife again, I'm going to loosen his bridgework a tooth at a time," Rafe said, his voice deceptively mild.

"What the hell are you talking about, boy? Bruno don't mess with fancy skirts." Emmett gave a harsh laugh.

"Bad choice of words, Dad," Rafe snarled, his body a menacing curve as he looked at his father.

"Eh?" Emmett looked open-mouthed at his eldest son. "I didn't mean anything personal. Don't be so damned touchy, boy."

"Good, then apologize to my wife for being tactless," Rafe offered, his voice having the hoarse sound it did when his temper was rising.

"Yeah? Well, all right, I apologize for the poor choice of words." Emmett broke his cigar, did a hundred-eighty-degree turn, and stalked away.

"You didn't have to upset your father because of me, Rafe." Cady felt as if multicolor balloons had gone off in her stomach. Rafe had never defended her against his father quite so decisively before. Although he'd been supportive of her verbally, there had always been a certain awe of his father that had undermined his words.

"Yes, I did." Rafe brushed his lips across her hair. "I never realized how he attacks you until my stay in the hospital, when I saw him at you whenever you met him. No wonder you always tried to be late so that you wouldn't run into him." He sighed as Trock signaled to him. "No time for a rest now. The fires are ready. Come along, lady, and watch me cook."

"I'll let you do a little if you promise that you'll sit

on the high stool while you do it." Cady felt her jaw push forward when Rafe grinned at her. "I mean it, Rafe. I won't let you tire yourself. The doctor says you're doing just fine, but he warned against overtaxing yourself."

"So my little angel has turned into a tyrant, is that it?" Rafe took one of the aluminum canes she held out to him and eschewed the other. "All right, boss lady, I'll use the stool while I'm doing the barbecuing, provided you stay at my side. Deal?"

"Deal." Cady laughed, feeling as light as a hot-air balloon when Rafe put his other arm around her and seemed to want her arm around him.

The cooking went well. The minute Trock thought Rafe had done enough, he insinuated himself into position as cook and eased Rafe back from the grills.

"That man is as high-handed as you are," Rafe grumbled, calling Graf to him. Cady followed Rafe's gaze. The dog had started to cross the lawn not far from where Bruno Trabold, now in a striped shirt of Rafe's, was talking to Emmett. "How did you get out here, boy?" Rafe rubbed the silken, pointed ears, glancing at Cady with a smile. "I remember when you brought him back with you after one of your stays with your father. He doesn't resemble that gaunt, frightened puppy anymore."

"No." Cady smiled down at the brown velvet dog, whose head cocked as though he could understand what his beloved people were saying. "If I hadn't been walking on the beach that day, he would have died out there. He couldn't get a grip on the ice to pull himself out of that frigid water," she remembered.

"What?" Rafe growled, his black brows snapping together, his blue eyes marble hard. "You never told me you went out on the ice after him. You just said you found him on the beach."

"Ah . . . well, no, I guess I didn't tell you I had to go out on the ice, but . . . ah, I was careful. I got the ladder from the boat house and pushed it in front of me. Graf was able to clutch the rungs with his paws and pull himself up. He was smart enough to stay on the ladder, and then I backed it toward me, easing my way on my stomach until I was on good solid ice."

Rafe grasped both her shoulders, numbing them. "Damn you, Cady, you could have died out there! You know what that lake is like when the ice backs up." He shut his eyes as though what he was seeing in his mind pained him. "When the ice melts, then refreezes, and the wind whips the open water onto the ice cap . . . God, Cady, it looks like the Alps on water. You know that." His eyes had darkened to indigo and seemed almost to be shooting sparks at her. "If you'd fallen in, no one would have seen you. You could have died. Don't ever be so stupid again."

The dog whined a question, making both of them look at him as he nosed between them.

"Don't worry, big boy, I wouldn't hurt your lady, but I'd like to paddle her derriere," Rafe rasped, gazing once more at Cady.

Cady felt daring. "You aren't strong enough yet, Senator, so be careful what you say. You might end up being paddled by *me*," she challenged, liking the martial light that flickered in his deep blue eyes.

"Threatening me, are you, wife?" Rafe crooned, his hand crawling up the inside of her right arm, his index finger touching her sensitive underarm.

Cady had no breath left. She felt her spine melt, her legs give way. It was an effort to keep her voice from squeaking. "Exactly. I intend to make you even stronger than you were before the accident, and if you try to spoil my plans . . . watch out." She lifted one small fist and shook it in his face.

"Let's go into the house and wrestle. The best two falls out of three wins," he drawled, his lips running from her temple to her jawline.

"Really, Cady, you might stop trying to seduce your husband in front of so many people," Lee Terris shrilled, making Emmett and Bruno laugh as the group moved toward them.

"Well, then hurry up and leave and I'll seduce him

in private," Cady simpered, wanting to take off her high-heeled sandal and hit the other woman with it.

Rafe roared at the three astonished faces looking at him. "Be careful, Lee, she's liable to throw you out of here." Rafe urged his wife forward. "Everyone seems to have some food. Let's get some for ourselves." Without another word to his father or the others, Rafe pointed to the table and smiled at Cady.

She was amazed at the way Rafe stayed at her side after eating, how often he included her in his conversation with other congressmen regarding his work, and how frequently he asked her opinion, his attention on her when she answered. She was flabbergasted at how many times he used the expression, "My wife thinks."

Still, they were separated a few times, and once when that happened, Rob Ardmore arrived at her side.

"Cady, I have to congratulate you on your handling of a very tricky political scene." He smiled down at her, not hiding the admiration in his eyes. "Rafe is a very lucky man. You made him look real good today."

"Rafe makes himself look good. People trust Rafe because they sense his strength, his commitment to the good of his state and of the country." Cady smiled at him, liking him.

"Spoken like a true politico's wife."

"I would prefer you to have said 'like a senator's wife.'" Cady grinned at him.

"If it ever gets tough, come to me, Cady. I'll be there for you," Rob whispered, lifting her hand to his mouth.

Suddenly Rafe appeared behind them.

"It's kind of you to be so concerned about my wife." His teeth were bared. "But I think I can take care of her now."

Cady's breath expelled in a sigh that was half sob. She hastened to explain. "Rob was a great help to me on the environmental bill, Rafe. He also put me in touch with the right lobbyists." She tried to hold that blue-ice gaze, but her lashes fluttered down. "Emmett and Bruno were at me all the time. Without Rob's help, I couldn't have done it. I don't have your knowledge of the Hill, Rafe."

"No." His voice was hard and uncompromising. He looked back at Rob Ardmore. "My wife won't be needing your assistance in the future."

Cady gasped. "Rafe, you have no right to tell me whom I can choose for my friends. I would never dare do such a thing with you, and I don't think you should with me." She ended on a shaky gulp, staring at the collar of his shirt instead of meeting his cold eyes.

"I see," he said stiffly, glancing from her to Rob. "Excuse me."

Cady gazed after him, misery pulsing through her body. She had been so happy earlier. They had seemed so much closer.

"Cady, don't look like that. The Densmores are a law unto themselves," Rob said, his voice soft. "No doubt no one in Rafe's whole life has spoken to him in such a fashion. I know I've never heard anyone answer him like that." Rob stepped closer. "Cady, will you be all right?"

"What did you say?" She looked up at him, his words scattering through her mind and then assembling. "Oh, yes, I'll be fine. Rafe is never mean to me. Don't worry about me."

"I do worry about you, Cady," he said as he turned to leave. "I can't help it."

Cady held out her hand to him. "Good-bye, Rob. I'm very glad you came today."

"Call me if you need me. Promise," Rob insisted.

"All right. If I ever need a friend, I'll call you." Cady forced a smile to her face.

Gradually the other guests drifted away. By the time the last ones had departed, Cady hadn't seen Rafe for almost two hours. He had been talking to Bruno, Emmett, and Lee Terris, but then that trio must have left, because she didn't see them again. Cady couldn't feel anything but relief that they hadn't bothered to say good-bye to her.

The late summer evening was turning deep purple as

she supervised the dismantling that the catering service was doing in the yard. By the time she entered the house, Trock was there to tell her that Rafe was in the sauna.

"Thank you, Trock. Tell the senator I said good night. Make sure that the oils are rubbed into his back tonight."

"Of course," Trock answered in a colorless voice.

Cady could see the flicker of reproach in Trock's gunmetal eyes. His gaze chided her that she would think he, Albert Trock, would forget such a thing. She touched his arm. "Good night, Trock, and thank you for all your help."

He inclined his head and left her. She sighed and began to ascend the curved stairway of the Federal-style colonial mansion. She trudged to her room, yawning, thinking only of the shower she would take.

When she came out of the shower into her bedroom, wrapped only in a bath towel, she staggered with shock when she saw Rafe sprawled on her bed, a blue toga around his middle. He rolled onto his side on the bed, facing her. "Hello. I think we have some unfinished business."

The unfathomable look was gone, and there was heated determination in his gaze. His jaw had the same granite look she had often seen before the accident, when he took the floor of the Senate and argued for a cause that he deemed just, an argument that brooked no rebuttal. The twist to his lips could be construed as a smile, but there was no softening there, no hint of compromise.

Cady's momentum carried her forward two more steps, then she stopped, clutching the bath towel like a shield. "You'd better go to bed. You need the rest," she told him, her tone crisp, belying the jellylike condition of her insides.

"You're not my doctor," Rafe answered in measured tones, swinging his legs to the floor.

Cady lifted her chin, gearing herself for battle. She had no idea which failed her first, her resolve or her knees. Panic filled her and she turned to run back to the bathroom. She had taken two steps when Rafe hooked her around the waist. "No, damn you, let me go," Cady squealed, a mixture of anger and sensual trepidation coming through her pores. "I'm not your concubine. I'm not your slave," she spit out through clenched teeth as she struggled to free herself.

"No, you're none of those things, but you are my wife, and I want my wife this evening," Rafe hissed, clamping her arms to her sides and pulling her back to the bed. "Behave yourself."

"No, I won't behave your way, damn it. If you need a woman, buy yourself one." Cady thrashed on the bed, his arm holding her while he divested himself of his robe. She stopped writhing when she saw the pinched look around his mouth, the strain sharpening the planes of his face. "You should go to bed. You've had a big day," Cady whispered as he lowered himself next to her.

"Isn't that what I've been saying?" Rafe let his head rest on her outspread hair, his hand coming up to globe one breast, his eyes closing. "Don't say you don't want me tonight, Cady. I'm dead tired, but I have to have you. It's been so long." His eyes fluttered open. "Even if I have to spend hours convincing you, I'm going to make you want me tonight."

Cady heard the little voice that told her he was just stringing her along, that he would dump her as soon as he could. She also heard the voice that told her he needed her tonight. Shutting her mind to everything but that, she lifted her arms to let her fingers touch the faint blue shadows under his even bluer eyes, smoothing the lines that pain had drawn down his cheeks. "Oh, I don't think it will take hours." She sighed and met his eyes.

"Cady?" Rafe growled softly, his hand going in tentative search at her breast as he pulled the towel free of her body. His hands rocked her close to him as he released a pent-up breath.

He leaned over her, his mouth opening on hers, his tongue running across her lips like a velvet letter opener. She welcomed the probe of his tongue like a hot knife on her senses. His body felt like an extended throb of her own, and it didn't seem like months since they had made love. It felt as though yesterday the same sensations had flowed through her. His mouth left hers to course down her body like a brand. "God, I have no control," Rafe said hoarsely. "I don't know how long...Oh, Cady, Cady..."

Her own body took fire at once, shocking her by the need that consumed her. She sensed his struggle to hold back so that she would be pleasured, and she became impatient with him. Didn't he know that she was burning for him? She let her hands feather over his body, provoking the heat in him. She became the aggressor as she heard him groan.

"Cady! Cady, I can't...Darling." He lifted himself over her, sensing her eagerness, surprised and pleased by her response. He played with her body as though she were a rare violin, his touch sure and arousing. Their coming together was blinding, their gasps loud in the stillness.

Rafe mumbled into her neck, but Cady couldn't understand the words. She was just sure that he didn't want her to move away from him. He was asleep almost at once.

Tired as she was, Cady couldn't sleep. There was much to think about, a life to plan. She and Rafe hadn't bothered about birth-control measures in a long time— not since the fifth year of their marriage. Then they had planned to start a family, and when no child had been conceived after a year of trying, Cady and Rafe went to their respective doctors for a thorough examination. The doctors had found no reason why the Densmores should not have the desired baby, yet still Cady didn't get pregnant. Secretly she blamed herself, and sometimes she wondered if Rafe underwent the same torment of doubt. In recent years their lovemaking had been so infrequent that it rarely occurred to Cady to calculate if she was fertile; her cycle was irregular anyway.

Certainly she had given no thought to getting pregnant since Rafe's accident. Nothing had intruded into her thoughts except Rafe's health and doing a good job for him in the Senate. She sighed as she cradled him to her. How ironic if she were to conceive now! Well, she wasn't going to use it as a lever if the miracle occurred, as she suspected was possible now. She would allow Rafe to get his divorce and she would raise the child herself. Rafe's child! How wonderful that would be! A smile curved her lips as she held him closer, her eyes fluttering shut.

In the morning Rafe was gone. Only the indentation on the pillow told Cady that last night hadn't been just a pleasurable dream. When she tried to rise, she felt the unaccustomed ache in her lower body, the heat rising into her face as she relived the eager abandon with which she had given herself to her husband.

She almost skipped to the bathroom, feeling the fulfilled happiness that had been a daily occurrence in the early days of their marriage.

She looked at the tub longingly and then glanced at her watch. She shrugged and sighed. It would have to be a fast shower.

She was singing "He Touched Me" off-key when she felt a cold draft. She tried to wipe the shampoo from her face to see who had opened the cubicle door when a warm hand began to wash her back.

"I thought for sure you would be able to stay on key after all the coaching I've given you." Rafe laughed as he brought the loofah sponge down over her derriere.

"If I had had a music minor in college as you did, I might have overcome that tiny deficiency." Cady tried to keep her voice level.

"Tiny deficiency!" Rafe pulled her back against him and reached around her to begin washing her front. He seemed to take eons with each breast. "There's a collection of cats waiting at the front gate. They think they've found their leader for an evening of caterwauling."

Cady wrestled the loofah from his hand and turned to face him, trying to shove the soapy sponge into Rafe's

mouth. "Caterwauler, am I? I'll show you." She struggled with him, wanting to see the soap froth from his
laughing mouth, but even without his full strength, Rafe
held her fast.

"Easy does it, angel." He chuckled, lifting her with
an arm under her buttocks so that they were face to face.
"Still think you can take me on, do you?" His tongue
flicked over her compressed lips.

"Yes," she gasped, loving every pore in his face, her
hand coming up to touch the fading scar on his jawbone
where he had been cut in the crash. She could remember
sitting next to his bed and counting each stitch in his
face, not really believing the plastic surgeon, Dr. Herra,
when he told her that the marks would fade. "You
shouldn't lift me the way you do. I'm too heavy, and
you're not strong enough yet," she mumbled, not sure
what she was saying.

"You're talking gibberish, do you know that?" Rafe
muttered, nibbling at her ear. "Are you lulling me into
a false sense of security?"

"Whatever." Cady bit at his chin and his cheekbones,
loving the feel of him.

"Are you going to make a meal out of me?"

"Maybe. Do you mind?" Cady felt glazed from head
to toe. She never wanted to leave the shower cubicle.

"No. I don't mind at all." Rafe's throat worked as
though he had swallowed a golf ball.

Cady felt a sense of triumph that he was as aroused
as she by their love play. Maybe she wouldn't be able
to keep him forever, she thought, but while she had him
she was going to love him.

Rafe pushed open the shower door and grabbed for a
bath towel, still holding her. She pouted when he had to
release her to wrap the towel around his waist.

He laughed down at her. "You look younger now than
you did at eighteen." He touched her lips with one finger.
"And don't pout like that or I'll take you here on the
bathroom floor."

Cady felt the heat start in her toes and course upward

until her entire being was on fire. "Are we going to talk all morning?"

"No." Rafe guffawed, sweeping her up into his arms. "We're going back to bed."

As they sank together on the bed, the interhouse phone rang.

"Damn them to hell," Rafe muttered, lifting the receiver and barking into it. "What? When? Well, you tell Bruno I said to head them off and he'd damn well better do it. Yes. Yes, damn it, I'm coming." Rafe slammed down the phone. "That was Sam Davis down at the office. It seems my father's friend Greeley has mounted an assault against the senators backing the environmental bill. According to Sam, he has some pretty big guns," Rafe mused, his hand still drawing imaginary whorls on her abdomen. "I have to get to the Hill."

"Of course," Cady agreed, edging away from him. "Would you like me to go with you?" she queried, trying to smother her frustrated longing. She was sure Rafe wouldn't want her along on one of the first big tests of his strength since taking back the reins of the senatorship.

"Yes, I'll want you with me, but more important, I want you back here, lady, not over there." Rafe reached for her, chuckling at her open mouth. "They can wait a few more minutes. Bruno can handle it." Rafe's mouth sank onto hers as though he had been drawn there by a homing device.

Cady could hear a purring sound as Rafe's head moved down her body. "Are you turning into a cat?" Rafe's laugh was uneven.

"Yes." Cady turned her body to his, reveling in arousing Rafe as he had aroused her.

"I think when I retire from public life, I'll take you away to a desert island," Rafe offered, seeming to be entranced with her navel.

"You'll get no argument from me," Cady choked, not really believing what she heard him say, but treasuring the words as though they were precious jewels.

Then there were no more words, just sensation after

sensation, like waves crashing on a shore. Cady heard him cry her name in a hoarse climax. The ebb tide of their love seemed almost as satisfying as the act itself, and Cady was loath to release him, not wanting to come back to the real world where Rafe would belong to other people, where as he became better he would be inundated in the river of persons that seemed to surround his every movement.

He rolled to his feet, pulling her with him, a lazy, sensuous look in his eyes as they roved over her body. "You were so tiny when I married you, but you're even smaller now." His fingers circled her waist as he led her to the bathroom. "You don't diet, do you Cady?"

"No." She wanted to tell him how pleased she was by his attention to her, but she turned toward the shower instead, mumbling that she would be right out. The quick, cold spray invigorated her without dispelling the glow that Rafe's lovemaking had given her.

His freshly shaved face turned from the mirror as she wrapped herself in a bath towel. "Of all your clothing, that suits you best." The sensual droop to his lower lip sent Cady's pulse racing.

She left the bathroom almost at a gallop, knowing that one word from Rafe and she would have dropped the towel and begged him to take her back to bed. Damn the man, she fumed to herself, she wouldn't let him rule her like that. She wasn't an eighteen-year-old girl anymore. She was a thirty-year-old woman. She could have run for the Senate. Cady looked in the dressing-table mirror as she applied a stroke of eyeliner. "And I could have won, too," she murmured out loud. She jabbed her pencil at the mirror. She had dealt well with those politicians. Even Rob Ardmore had said so.

All at once she put her face in her hands, moaning. Yes, but what would she do when Rafe didn't want her? Her head jerked up, her luminous violet eyes glittering with anger. Don't be a fool! she admonished herself. You can have a life! You can go to Greece and work in the digs. You were going to be a working archaeologist. You still can.

She nodded her head at her image, accepting the nebulous comfort of her arguments. Then she stood surveying herself in the long mirror. The velvet corduroy suit in palest orchid with a weskit instead of a jacket and with a deeper orchid long-sleeve blouse should have had a spring look, but instead it had the purplish haze of the autumn color of upstate New York after the leaves have fallen. Her shoes were a champagne suede with a matching shoulder bag. She left her long hair down, swinging on her shoulders.

"Well, well. Is this what the well-dressed interim senator usually wears?" Rafe drawled from the doorway, both hands at his hips, pushing his suit jacket back from his body.

"Do you like it?" Cady tried to keep the breathiness from her voice, but Rafe's blue eyes made her dizzy.

"Very much. It's the sexiest utilitarian garment I've ever seen, and it makes your eyes look purple," he observed, reaching for her arm to lead her down the stairs.

"Isn't it unusual to call a gathering of senators on the Hill on Sunday?" Cady stopped in the doorway leading out to the patio, where a light lunch was waiting for them.

"It's not senators." Rafe smiled at her. "Some lobbyists representing chemical firms and the nuclear power people want me to pull in my horns about clean water and air." His lips curled. "I imagine they don't want much . . . just that I keep my mouth shut and not support those bills that my wife fought so hard to keep alive for me." He looked down at her and his face turned grim for a moment, a hard, faraway look coming into his eyes. "The lobbyists have enlisted Bruno Trabold's help in bringing me to heel."

"All against the environment, of course," Cady observed, recalling the pressures that had come to bear against her when she had decided that the very life and breath of the planet were being endangered. What had once been an interest became an absorption when she discovered how careless many were about the atmosphere when they pursued the dollar.

"Yes," Rafe said, leaning toward her. "You know, Cady, my hearing was never impaired in the accident, and I listened when you talked about what was being done to our country in the name of progress. I remember how appalled you were about the goings-on in our state. I learned a great deal from you, wife."

She could feel her face go pink with pleasure at the earnestness in his voice. How lovely to hear him praise her, to know that he had paid so much attention to what she said. She thought she might even enjoy this meeting on Capitol Hill.

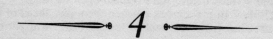

4

THE CAPITOL WAS bathed in sunlight, its concrete facade having a pinkish hue that looked welcoming on the crisp autumn day. As usual, tourists lined the steps of the many buildings along Constitution Avenue. The sight never failed to delight Cady. As though Rafe could read her mind, he ordered their driver to slow the vehicle on the wide, parklike avenue.

When Rafe noticed people looking at the car with curiosity, he waved to some children, who waved back. When their parents bent to them and whispered, then pointed to the car, Rafe asked the chauffeur to stop the limousine.

Cady knew Rafe was sincerely interested in people, especially children. She felt a wrench as she thought of the decision they had made long ago not to have children right away because they wanted more time with each other. Cady often speculated that she might have conceived more easily at eighteen, and perhaps if they had had children at once they might have been able to avert

63

the rift that had developed between them. She wondered now if they would ever have offspring, and if not, would it be her fault? She sighed and put the thought from her mind, smiling at the youngsters who had run up to the car.

Rafe seemed to have limitless patience as he answered their questions and told them that he thought that Kansas, their state, was quite beautiful and that he was fond of sunflowers.

They left the children and were driven to the entrance at the back. They took the elevator to Rafe's office, which had been Cady's office for many months. She could hear Bruno's voice before Rafe pushed open the door.

"Rafe." Bruno's croak reached them just ahead of his outstretched hand. He leaned toward Rafe, whispering, "You'll have to back down some. These boys mean a lot of blocks in the voting booths." His eyes shifted to Cady, but he didn't speak to her.

She shivered and stepped closer to Rafe.

Rafe waded into the group, talking and smiling. For an instant Cady felt her faith in him waver. Would he be coerced by his father's political cronies into defeating the latest environmental bill? Then she heard the man called Greeley whine, "Listen, Rafe, you'd better back down. If I tell my people you ain't comin' across"—he shrugged, wiping one hand down his overstuffed jacket—"you'll lose enough votes to put you out of a job."

The others muttered loudly, nodding.

"I'm not backing down," Rafe announced, pulling a pencil-slim cigar from a flat case. "I'm just not contributing to the health problems of my constituents because you want a cheap way to dump chemicals. Forget it. My wife made an in-depth study of chemical dumping, and I'm against the method you're lobbying for."

"Then the men I've got will bury you, Rafe," Greeley growled.

Cady stepped forward to her husband's side. "And the women in the Coalition to Protect Our Children will hear about you, Mr. Greeley. We'll stump the state and tell every mother and father we can that you wish to kill their children in a very protracted and painful way." She lifted her chin. "I wouldn't be surprised if the women lynched you, sir. We're through letting people like you destroy our state. If you try to cross my husband, you'll find that we hit back, too . . . and hard." Cady could feel her knees quaking, and she laced her moist hands together to conceal their tremors.

"Feisty broad, aren't ya? Emmett told me you were a troublemaker." Greeley wet his thick lips with his tongue.

Rafe leaned forward, putting his index finger into the middle of Greeley's corpulent belly. "If you ever call my wife a broad again, Greeley, I'm going to put my fist where this finger is," he announced conversationally, his smile widening when the man retreated a step. "I don't think I have to repeat what Cady just said. If you want a fight, you'll get one." Rafe stepped away from his desk. "Get out of here. You're ruining my Sunday."

The men filed out, still muttering.

Bruno stood to one side of the open door. "You're making a mistake getting their backs up like that, Rafe. Emmett won't like it, and you'll weaken your own position in the party."

"Cut the crap, Bruno." Rafe's face was as harsh as his voice. "No matter what you or my father thinks, my political leverage has never depended on men like Greeley. I've never underestimated him, but I'm not afraid of him, either."

"Damn it, Rafe, you used to be smarter than this!" Bruno all but shouted. "Greeley knows a lot about you— your early days in the House. Remember those parties he arranged? Remember the trouble you had . . . ?" Bruno flicked a hard look at Cady, then shrugged.

Cady could feel Rafe standing rigidly at her side. She flashed a quick glance at him, seeing the red staining his neck and crawling up his cheeks. His face looked hewn from granite. She cleared her throat. "If you're referring to the party at Durra when the highway patrol were called and it was discovered that the youngest congressman from the state of New York was hosting a party of call girls and other congressmen—if you're referring to the writeup in *The Tattler* with pictures of said congressman frolicking in his father's pool with a cheesecake blonde and that both were nude—if that's what you mean, Bruno, then speak up and don't worry about me. I know most of the details." Cady sensed that Rafe had kept his eyes on her profile from the moment she began to speak. She knew he didn't see Bruno bare his teeth at her in rage.

"All right, Cady, so you know what can be done to defeat Rafe's reelection," Bruno growled softly. "Are you going to let some bleeding hearts destroy your husband's future when with just a little cooperation, he could win?"

"Shut up, Bruno, and don't try to coerce Cady. I won't allow it. If Greeley tries to heat up those old ashes, I'll leak to the press that it was Greeley himself and his boys who hired those women to descend on Durra. What do you think people will think of that sort of thing? I'll tell the world that this is the way Mr. Greeley does business. Do you think it will do Emmett's name any good to be linked to a gigantic call girl ring, with his friend Mr. Greeley as procurer?"

"You don't know what you're taking about," Bruno snarled at the same time that Rafe moved from Cady's side toward his father's aide.

"Don't I?" Rafe looked from Bruno to Cady, the flicker deep in those blue eyes telling her how painful this was for him. He grabbed Bruno's shirt front. Then, like a flash, he looked back at Cady. "How the hell do you know so much about this?"

Cady thought her smile must make her look as if she'd sucked a lemon. "There were more than enough people on the Hill willing to tell me all about my rakish husband and his high-flying days after his first election. Most of them put it down to your being just another one of those wild Densmores—bright, but wild," Cady finished, her throat feeling tight.

"Cady, for God's sake . . ." Rafe began, turning his back on Bruno.

"And"—Cady lifted her left hand palm outward as though to forestall his words—"I also was made very aware that it was one of those parties you were heading toward when the plane crashed on the way to Durra. I can't tell you how many kind people came forward to inform me what a real good-time Charlie I had married," she concluded, sarcasm in her voice as she fought to keep the searing pain from showing.

"Cady, I swear to you—" Rafe began hoarsely.

"For goodness sake, don't perjure yourself, Rafe," Cady said, gulping.

"Cady, listen to me—" he barked.

Bruno's laugh bellowed into the room. "I guess you can't fool the missus, Rafe."

Rafe turned and swung at the same time, his right fist catching Bruno on the point of his jaw, the crunch of bone against bone a sickening sound.

Bruno was strong and thickset, but he reeled back against the filing cabinet, his head snapping back. "Why, you . . ." he rasped, putting his hands up like a street fighter, ready to come at Rafe.

"Come on, Bruno. Do it. There's nothing I want more than to pull you apart," Rafe vowed thickly, his body curving in menace, obviously with no regard for his physical welfare.

"Stay and fight, but let me out of here," Cady said, her voice shrill as she pushed at Rafe in an effort to get past him. "And . . . and don't you dare have a relapse from fighting," she choked.

"Cady, don't. Wait for me. We have to talk," Rafe insisted, his attention focusing on her again.

"No, I'm leaving. Stay away from me." Cady didn't look at Bruno again as she stumbled from the room.

She heard the low voices and knew Rafe was saying something to Bruno, but she was too busy running to care. An elevator was standing open and she jumped into it, punching the button for the lobby.

When she ran down the steps of the office building, a taxi was just discharging a passenger. She hailed it and told the cabbie to drive to Virginia.

She leaned back against the upholstery of the taxi cab, pressing her fingertips into her eyes. Why had she said all that? Her mouth had let go like a ruptured dam, spilling all the bitter truths that she had hugged to herself for so long. Rafe had never known that she was aware of the details of the scandal at Durra, his father's palatial estate in the horse country of Maryland. She sighed as she remembered the atomic row they had had in the early days of their marriage when she told Rafe that she wouldn't accompany him to a lawn party his father was hosting at Durra. She had been young and too hurt by the freshness of the disclosure that Stacy Lande, then a secretary in Bruno's office, had made during a benefit to aid battered children that they were attending.

"But Cady, honey, you're so naive," Stacy had said uneasily. "I was just kidding about old news. I wasn't trying to hurt you. Many big guns politico-wise were there." Stacy had become increasingly uncomfortable. It isn't so bad for you, really. You didn't even know Rafe then. Honey, I wish you wouldn't look like that. It's all water over the dam. Honestly, Cady, I never meant to hurt you."

"It's all right," Cady had lied. "I'm not a bit hurt. Of course, I knew that Rafe was quite a lady's man." She had smiled and buried the pain.

She realized, now that she was older, that if she had faced Rafe then with what she had discovered and they had talked about it, it might not have mushroomed in her mind. Instead she found herself looking at Rafe when he wasn't watching her, wondering what he was like with other women when she wasn't there. Then she would berate herself, telling herself that she knew Rafe had seen other women before he met her, but also that she had no reason to believe that he had ever been unfaithful to her.

For a long time things seemed to go back on even

keel between them, but then Rafe was gone for long periods of time and bitter arguments had ensued. Cady smiled ruefully when she remembered that it hadn't been other women that had sparked the tiffs but angry confrontations when Rafe listened to his father and Bruno about not supporting nuclear regulatory legislation and enviromental protection bills. More often than not Cady found herself at odds with both Bruno and her father-in-law. Rafe resented it when she accused his father of callousness vis-à-vis the good of the state and being interested only in his own markets and those of his friends.

Great gulfs were gouged between them. Eventually, Cady remembered, there had seemed to be no safe topic they could discuss without beginning to argue hotly. There were long periods of silence between them. Soon they began to see different cliques of people. Cady threw herself into volunteer work while still keeping abreast of the newest methods in archaeology, the life's work she would have chosen had she continued into the master's program. She grinned wryly as she remembered how, after they were married, she had enrolled at Georgetown in her original major of physics, and how Professor Feinbloom had channeled her enthusiasm toward his own field of archaeology. She had fully intended to get her master's and had begun the courses for the three years it would take her at the pace she had set herself. She had been careful to take an underload so that nothing would interfere with her duties as a senator's wife.

After the accident, when she had taken over the duties of Rafe's office, it had been archaeology that had drawn her to Rob Ardmore, when she discovered that he had dabbled in the field himself while at the university.

Cady looked out the window of the cab and wondered what her life with Rafe would have been like if only she had been mature enough to go to him when she was troubled. Would he have been so resentful of her attitude toward his father if he had realized how obstructive Emmett was with her? Would he have believed her if she had told him when she first discovered that Bruno and Emmett manipulated him for their own political reasons?

She smiled humorlessly as the cab turned into the long, curving drive that led to her house. How ironic, she thought, that the only time she ever fully communicated with Rafe was when he was lying helpless in a tilted bed, unable to respond!

She paid the cab and looked up at the facade of the Mount Vernon–type house. She had always liked this house because of its spacious airiness, but all at once she longed for the quiet anonymity of their home in upstate New York. She wanted to see her father again. She wanted to feel the balm of his wisdom, his soft humor.

In that moment she made up her mind. She was going home.

With sudden intuition she knew that Rafe would try to stop her. He wouldn't like her going. He never liked that. He could go off on fact-finding tours throughout the state or the world and he expected Cady to accept that, but he hated it when she left him to visit her father. The one time she had accompanied a friend to New York City to see a new musical that everyone had raved about, he had muttered into his soup for days afterward.

She greeted the ecstatic Doberman who raced around the house to greet her, Trock at his heels.

"Everything straightened out, Mrs. Densmore?" Trock watched her, his face expressionless.

"The senator is handling it, but I think he has a fight on his hands." She rubbed the silken ears of the dog as they turned toward the rose garden in unspoken agreement. Cady's nostrils distended as she inhaled the sweetness around her. The roses were dying back now but had taken on a new luster because of the cool overnight rain. The mild Virginia weather would sometimes let them bloom until November.

"He'll beat 'em as soon as he has you riding shotgun for him, Mrs. D.," Trock said, his sandpaper voice sounding strained after disgorging so many words.

Startled, Cady turned to look at the man, wondering if the taciturn Trock was being sarcastic.

"You're his good right arm, Mrs. D. Didn't you know that?"

Cady shook her head, unable to accept what he was saying.

"Believe it, Mrs. D." Trock coughed as though his throat was so out of condition for talking that he had to keep clearing the debris of words. "He's got nobody else but you . . ." He looked down at the dog, who was leaning against Cady's legs. "And of course Graf here . . . and me."

Cady smiled at the laconic man facing her across a huge Peace rosebush that had the circumference of a good-size dining room table. "Trock, the senator has a large family here in Virginia. He has cousins in Texas and Florida. He's very close to his brothers and sisters."

"He's close to them, true, but they aren't close to him." He breathed hard. "I saw plenty at the nursing home, Mrs. D. You came to see him every day. Not the rest of them, though; they didn't come so regularly. Oh, I know they told you at the desk they came, but Mr. Emmett and Mr. Trabold actually came about once a week, a little more sometimes. The twins came a couple times a week, the sisters maybe twice a month. Then they'd sit there and spill their guts about all their troubles."

Cady stared at him, aware that her mouth was agape. "You're saying that all those times when I hurried to leave so that Rafe could spend some time with family members . . . ? You mean they didn't visit according to the schedule? That it was all a sham? That I could have stayed as long as I wanted to?"

"Most days, yes, ma'am, I'd say that. I wanted to say something, but I thought maybe you had set up the schedule yourself."

"I didn't. Bruno Trabold insisted that Emmett and the family wanted to have their own time with Rafe, so I agreed to a schedule." Cady felt her voice choke. "You

mean that many times he spent all those hours alone with
no one to visit him?"

"Yes, ma'am. That's when I got into the habit of
playing chess with him. He would blink once for yes
and twice for no when I moved the pieces. He was a
smart cuss, even strapped to that bed."

"Oh, Lord," Cady moaned. "I would have spent every
moment with him." She bit her lip, fighting back tears.
"Thank you, Trock, for not abandoning him, but oh, I
wish I'd known."

"No sense looking back." He harumphed again. "That's
why when I heard you talking to the senator about having
the operation, I knew it was the right thing to do. I knew
he wanted it."

"Yes," Cady whispered.

"Then you must know how much he'll need your help
with this environmental thing he was talking about.
Right?" Trock persisted, just about through with talking
for the day.

Cady stared at the stocky attendant, knowing that his
medium build was deceptive, that he was strong and
muscular. She let her glance rove from the steel-gray
crew cut to the masklike face and down the dungaree-
clad body. Had he read her mind? Did he suspect that
she wanted to leave and go home? Did Rafe really need
her as much as Trock said he did?

"I don't know what the bills are all about...but I
know he needs your help." Trock inhaled deeply.

"I think you mean the environmental bill that Harold
Long, another senator, is cosponsoring. That's the legislation that Greeley's men are fighting."

Trock nodded. "I guess that's it," he said. "Listen,
Mrs. D., are you and the senator dining in tonight?"

"What? Dining in? Oh, yes, I feel it's better not to
have activities back-to-back for the senator. That way he
doesn't tire as much..." Cady's voice faltered, her mind
jumbled and going in all directions.

"Good idea. The senator is getting stronger every day.

He'll be better than he was before when I get through
with him."

Cady put her hand on Trock's arm. "I hope for all
our sakes you will never consider yourself done with the
senator, but whatever you decide, I want you to know
you will always have a home with us."

Blood chugged into Trock's face, and his mouth and
throat worked as though he were trying to digest a two-
by-four. He nodded once at Cady, then turned away,
striding toward the barnlike building that housed the therapy equipment.

Graf whined at her side, drawing Cady's attention.

"All right, boy." She patted him in an absent fashion,
walking in a tangent toward the open french doors leading
from the library. "Let's go for a swim," she told the
happy dog as he padded next to her up the stairs, the
nails on his paws clacking like typewriter keys.

It took mere minutes to don her one-piece bathing
suit, reach for a terry-cloth wrap, and hurry down the
stairs again.

The pool was a regulation twenty-five-yard rectangle
that could be fitted with a bubble when the weather turned
cold. An avid swimmer, Cady used the pool every day
she could.

Graf had begun jumping in the pool at Rafe's coaxing
when Rafe had come home from the hospital. Now the
dog was in the habit of swimming with Cady or Rafe.
Cady assumed the dog swam with Trock as well, but she
had never seen them in the pool together.

She was on her thirtieth lap, her goggles a little steamed
up, when she felt the roll and splash of the water that
told her someone else had entered the pool. She stopped
swimming for a moment, treading water easily, and pushing the goggles back on her head to look around her.
She felt a feathery touch on her stomach, and before she
could react, she was pulled under, Rafe's grinning face
in front of her. Continuing to blow bubbles of air through
his nose, he pulled her close to his body and clamped

his legs over hers. They surfaced, still kissing.

Cady leaned back, gasping for air. "Do you have an auxiliary tank built into your lungs?" she gulped at him, frowning.

He held her easily, suspended in his arms. "Are you angry with me, Cady? I guess I always knew that you would discover the scandal at Durra, but I hoped you wouldn't." Rafe released her to let her float on her back, his arm supporting her and her head on his shoulder. "It's something I deeply regret, and I could never bring myself to speak of it to you. I wanted you to be proud of me."

"I was very proud to marry you, Rafe." Cady's voice had a tremor in it.

"But not too proud when you heard about Durra," he said flatly, his hand tightening under her breasts. "Cady, I won't try to make excuses for myself..."

Cady rolled free of him, splashing them both, then stroked to the side of the pool.

"Cady, wait. Let's talk." His long arms touched the side of the pool at almost the same time as Cady's.

"There's nothing to talk about, Rafe." Her voice wobbled. "Bruno only hammered home the facts I've tried not to admit to myself." She turned to look at him, locking her jaw to keep her face from crumpling into tears. "You were on your own for a long time before you met me. You traveled around the world and you moved with a very slick crowd. I knew that, but I still foolishly thought that I would be enough for you."

"You were, Cady." Rafe bit off the words. "You still are."

Her head swung back and forth like a pendulum. "No, Rafe, don't you fall into that trap, believing the fairy story of our marriage that you used in your campaign material."

"Cady, I have been faithful to you," he growled, sweeping back his wet hair with one hand.

"Have you?" She shivered as much from the chill of the air on her wet body as from the shock of memory. "On the day the plane crashed, you were on your way to Durra. Bruno and Emmett told me while I waited in the hospital corridor for the doctor to come and tell me that you had died."

"Did you wish that I had? Died, I mean?" Bitterness laced Rafe's voice, and his nostrils were pinched white.

"Damn you!" Cady blazed, raising herself out of the pool, a trembling hand reaching for the terry-cloth robe. "Is that what you think?" She whirled to face him, temper igniting her body like a match to spilled gasoline. "I won't try to change your mind, but kindly remember that I spent many long hours in office work, in caucus, in meetings, trying to keep your seat...and...then...then I came to visit you..." Her breath rasped out of her throat in painful jerks. Hot tears that she had buried for too long seemed to well up like a boiling geyser. "And ...don't you think...I'm crying. Because I'm not... and...don't you come near me...ever again." She tried to whirl away from him, But Rafe caught her wrist.

"Forgive me, Cady, please. It was a stupid thing to say and I didn't mean it." He took a deep breath. "Cady, shall I tell you what I remember, what made me hang on in that living hell?"

She didn't turn to look at him or even nod, but she stopped trying to struggle free.

"There were so many special moments, but the one that still comes back in my dreams was the day you were sitting sprawled in the easy chair. Your eyes were closed and you were limp with fatigue, yet you described the day you had had fighting for the Mead-Sligh reclamation bill that would allow people who had been affected by chemical waste to have recourse to instant financial help. Then you started to mumble about the other things that you were determined not to let slip, other bills that I was interested in that you had listed in order of importance to me." His hand tightened on her wrist. "You still had your eyes closed, but you were smiling and you said, 'I'll tread softly over your dreams, Rafe, I promise. Do you remember that quotation by Yeats, darling?' Then you fell sound asleep."

He tugged gently but insistently on her wrist, turning her to face him. "I remember the quotation, Cady, because as soon as I could use my hands, I looked it up in *Bartlett's*. 'I have spread my dreams under your feet; Tread softly, because you tread on my dreams.' That's it, isn't it, Cady?" He was whispering now.

"Yes, that's it." Cady felt as though each word she said were wrenched from her throat.

"Cady, the dreams I had for our state and for the country are still alive in me. If you can't believe in me as a husband, will you believe in me as a senator and help those dreams come true? I need you in the coming election."

"I know that." Cady tried to mask the hurt that his words caused. She wanted to yell at him, shake him, force him to want her as a woman—not as the senator's wife.

"Will you help me, Cady?"

"I'll help you to achieve your aims, because I believe in them, too, but I won't . . ."

Rafe put his finger to her lips. "Don't say any more. We'll just go with what we've got." His lips curved in a twist of a smile. "We'll give them a hell of a run for their money in this election, won't we, Cady?"

5

THE CAMPAIGN SWUNG into high gear almost at the moment of their return to New York. Cady was rather startled to find that she was well known to so many of Rafe's constituents. Many even called her by name. Even more astonishing to her was that she enjoyed accompanying Rafe and talking to the people. She had never considered herself an extrovert, but her months of working in Rafe's Senate office had whittled down the rough edges of her shyness. She tried to explain this metamorphosis to her father one evening when Rafe was dining with some of his political strategists in the area. She had taken advantage of the brief respite to visit with the professor.

"It's incredible, Father, really!" She smiled at him, taking note of the piercing stare that seemed to see through her. "All those years at school when I would tremble and shake over giving reports and taking oral exams, and now I'm meeting hundreds of people at once and carrying it off. Amazing, isn't it?"

"Amazing," Professor Nesbitt echoed, his tone dry. He tapped his pipe against his left palm, not taking his eyes from her. "We've skirted any discussion of you all evening, my darling daughter," he observed, filling the pipe with slow, measured movements. "And though I'm fully in accord with my son-in-law's aims—in fact I'm most curious about his new wariness toward the Greeley people he had in his camp—for the moment I would like to hear about you. You have shadows under your eyes, Cady. What's wrong?"

"Nothing, Father," she choked, trying to keep her smile in place. "The campaign is tiring, of course, and I don't look as sharp as I should . . ."

"It's not your looks, even though you are too thin. That happened after Rafe's accident, and I can understand it. It was a very rough time for both of you; but that crisis is past. What's bothering you now, Cady? I see the hurt etched into your face and I don't like that. Do you want to talk about it?" Her father's voice was gentle, as always, but Cady detected a thread of steel in it. "I knew there would be pain for you," he went on, "marrying a man like Rafe, but you loved him so much." He shrugged, a bitter lift to his mouth.

"I still do," Cady choked, wanting to talk with her father but unable to confide to anyone that Rafe didn't love her and would, perhaps soon, be asking her for a divorce. "I'm not trying to fool you, Father. It's only that speaking about the problems between Rafe and me makes me so miserable."

"Then you admit there are problems." Her father's voice was gruff.

"There are problems in every marriage. You know that." Cady's mouth felt like rubber as she tried to smile.

"All right, child; but promise me you'll come to me if things get *too* rough."

"I promise, Father."

"Now tell me about this Greeley thing. Where did all the bully boys go who used to be on the fringe of Rafe's camp?" Professor Nesbitt's eyes sharpened when her lips curved upward.

"Rafe was a tiger with them. Bruno Trabold made the tactical mistake of trying to back Rafe into a corner on an issue." Cady kept her eyes on her father's chin, determined not to give him any details about the Durra scandal, even though she sensed that he knew more about Rafe than he let on. "Bruno underestimated Rafe's fighting ability and overplayed his hand. When he revealed that Greeley had been trying to manipulate Rafe, Rafe came out of his corner like a pit terrier," she finished, her lips a straight line.

"Speaking of pit terriers," her father said, tamping his pipe, "I understand from the newspapers that my daughter has entered the fray on the side of the Society for Prevention of Cruelty to Animals to protect that great species of canine from being exploited in illegal fighting."

Cady leaned forward in her chair, two coin-size spots of red high in her cheeks. "Dad, if you could see what happens to these dogs when they're thrown into one of those fights, it would make you sick. They are literally torn to pieces." Her chin thrust forward. "And just as Rafe rid himself of the Greeley faction, I'm going to help sweep that disgusting so-called sport from our state."

Professor Nesbitt's stern face softened, his eyes twinkling. "I would certainly run if you came at me with that martial light in your eye. You're quite a tiger yourself, Cady."

At that moment Rafe strolled into the room, his charcoal pin-strip suit looking as fresh as when he left that morning. Both Cady and her father started—they had been so absorbed in their conversation that they hadn't heard the click of Rafe's key in the front door lock.

"No truer words were ever spoken, Thomas." Rafe chuckled, pulling his tie free from his neck as he stood in the doorway. "You haven't seen your daughter in action in the political arena yet. Why don't you come to the luncheon the Monroe County women are hosting for Cady? She's making a speech that day. The first time I heard her speak, I didn't even listen to the words. I was too busy watching the way she curled the audience right into her palm. She's a marvel." Her husband's voice brimmed with pride.

Cady had heard Rafe praise her often during the campaign, but it never failed to stir her, to make the blood rise in her face as it did now. "Rafe, you've already invited the world to this rally. I hope I won't fall on my face."

"That's false modesty and you know it, wife. Even Clem Martin, my campaign manager, said that you are my greatest asset." He walked across the room to lean down and brush her lips with his. This had become a habit of Rafe's whenever they greeted each other or parted. Cady knew that it was a mechanical gesture to him, but for her it was a heart-wrenching experience, and she treasured every caress. Still, it became increasingly hard to disguise the effect he had on her, especially since her hands ached to reach for his neck and clutch him to her.

"I think I will come." Professor Nesbitt pursed his lips, a faraway look in his eyes. "Yes, I could drive up in the morning."

"No, Thomas, I'll send the plane for you," Rafe corrected. "It's a beautiful ride up the lake. Then you could stay with us in the city and fly back the next morning."

"Oh, please do it, Father. I'd like it so much." Cady felt her throat constrict. "It would bolster my confidence."

"I thought I was supposed to do that," Rafe observed, his tone wry.

Cady gave him a quick glance, noting the opaque look of his eyes. "Of course you do. But I'd like my father to be there, too."

"Of course." He looked past her to the professor. "We should be leaving, Thomas. It's a fifteen-mile drive to the house and then it's early to rise tomorrow."

"Then why not stay here for the night? It might make

it easier for you if I flew into the city with you in the morning instead of sending the plane for me." Professor Nesbitt was studying the bowl of his now-extinguished pipe as though such a scrutiny were crucial.

"Father, no!" Cady exclaimed in horror, trying to catch the professor's eye. "My clothes! I have to . . . to get my things . . . and . . ."

"Nonsense, child, you have clothes here and more in the city if you need them, and you have your briefcase with your speech with you." He looked over his half-glasses, his lips firm. "You should set an example for energy conservation and not take two plane trips when you can take one."

Rafe gave a dry laugh. "Your father's right, Cady. We'll stay the night." His dark brows arched even further at the glowering look she gave him. "I'm for a shower and bed." He turned away, striding from the sitting room. The muffled thumps as he climbed the stairs were loud in the stillness.

"Father, I . . ." Cady cleared her throat.

"Cady, I wouldn't dream of interfering in your life, but I will tell you this. If you want to keep your husband and your marriage, then make up your mind to fight for them. If you don't care, then forget what I said." Professor Nesbitt rose to his feet, stretching. "I think I'll turn in as well. Good night, child."

"Good night, Father. I think I'll make myself a hot lemon and honey to relax me." She knew her smile was a feeble attempt, but she wanted time to think.

She stood at the stove, stirring the boiling water into the lemon and honey mixture, arguing silently with herself. Big deal! You'll be sleeping with your husband! But I haven't been sleeping with him since we came back to New York, she argued back. So? Her inner demon prodded. Go to bed and forget about it. Rafe's probably sound asleep. Why did she think he was so concerned about her? Wasn't he just waiting for the right time to suggest that they divorce?

She swallowed the last of her hot drink and nodded

her head, agreeing with the last thought. She rinsed out the cup and left it on the drainboard.

As she climbed the stairs she inhaled the smells and sensations that emanated from the old house. She could almost hear her own laughter when she and a childhood friend had slid down the curving oak banister.

She hurried into the small bathroom that opened onto the hall and also into the bedroom that had been hers as a girl. She knew that Rafe would be in her double bed with the white eyelet canopy and dust ruffle to match. He would not want to give Mrs. Tibbs anything to gossip about when she came to make up the rooms tomorrow, so he would expect no fuss from her.

She dawdled over brushing her teeth and washing her face. Tonight she would try to find one of her old nightgowns. Since her marriage to Rafe, she had gotten into the habit of sleeping nude, but she wouldn't do that tonight.

She padded into the bedroom clad only in her bra and panties, finding her way easily in the dark room. She grabbed for the first garment at hand and grimaced when she discovered it was a high-neck, long-sleeve flannel nightie that she had worn in her early college days.

She sighed as she slipped it over her head after removing her undergarments, knowing she would feel like an uncomfortable bundle.

She edged into bed, then lay there as stiff as a board, clinging to her side of the bed. Just as she was beginning to relax, having decided that Rafe must be asleep, she felt the bed move and sag as he turned and reached for her.

"Sorry to disappoint you. I'm awake, Cady. And I'm going to hold you," he grated next to her ear.

"It's late," she murmured, loving the feel of his arms tightening around her yet determined not to let him discover how much she wanted him to hold her, not just tonight but for all the nights and all the days of her life.

"Cady, my little love, it's never too late for what I have in mind," Rafe mumbled into her neck, his teeth taking small nibbles at the cord in the side of her neck. "You're like a luscious, tantalizing dessert that I can't resist. Tonight I'm going to make a feast of you, my Cady."

"You're crazy," she gasped. "People aren't meals."

"You're ambrosia to me." Now Rafe's voice was guttural as he slid the nightie over her head. "When did you start wearing horse blankets to bed?" he muttered, raising himself back from her to look at her body in the pale light of the moon as it filtered through the sheer curtains at the window. "You still have the same perfect body you had at eighteen. It amazes me that you look the same." His hands followed his eyes down the length of her, his lips taking on a more sensual droop before his mouth dropped to her navel. "I love your body, darling."

Cady reacted to the endearment like a drawn bow, arching toward him. She reached toward his head, threading her fingers through his hair, wanting to keep him close.

Before she could say anything, he had lifted his head, sliding up her body, his lips urgent on hers. There was an angry need in his mouth and body, the hunger building there as though he had been banked like a fire that had now erupted into flame.

She forgot all the reasons why she shouldn't let him touch her. Everything was forced from her senses but her overwhelming need of him. Heated tremors racked her form as every cell in her body reached out to him. The tactile delight she enjoyed as her fingers molded his skull made her dizzy. The warning voice that came from deep inside her was not heeded. She was in the grip of a white heat of desire and longing that erased all reason.

Their coming together was as explosive as the last time after the barbecue at the Highlands. Cady dropped off to sleep almost at once, hazily aware that she was still held close to Rafe.

In the morning she felt shy with him. She wasn't able to hold his glance when she spoke to him, but she was aware of the heat in his look. It was the same expression that had always been on Rafe's face when he looked at her in the early days of their marriage, before arguments and misunderstandings replaced it with an opaque, aloof cast to his eyes.

She dressed with great care for the luncheon, donning a cranberry wool suit with a short hip-length jacket and a straight skirt. She wore black calf shoes with a matching grip bag. Her blouse was ecru silk with fine cranberry lines threaded through the fabric. Just before it was time to leave for the event, which was to be held at one of the local hotels in Monroe County, she closeted herself in her room and pored over her speech, which she had prepared herself. She never let anyone else write her speeches, though she always let one of the election aides proofread them for her.

The second knock at the door penetrated her consciousness. "Yes? Come in."

"Ready, Cady?" Rafe stood there in a familiar stance. His hands were shoved into his pockets, his jacket thrust backward. His eyes narrowed as she rose to her feet, taking in her outfit and the blood creeping up her cheeks. "Intelligent persons are almost always a little bit nervous before speeches. I am." His grin was cheeky. "And don't say that I'm not intelligent or you'll damage my ego."

"I won't say that. I'll just say that you have an ego the size of a hot-air balloon," Cady observed, appreciating his attempt to keep her relaxed.

"Really?" Rafe's teeth snapped together in a wolfish grin. He strolled toward her. "Very disloyal remark, Mrs. Densmore."

Cady wasn't fooled by the bland tone, and she watched him warily. "We'll be late," she warned, stepping back.

Rafe's arm moved to imprison her before Cady could move again. "Conceited, am I?" He lowered his mouth to her neck.

"Very," Cady breathed, feeling his hands clasp her waist.

"It's bad form to insult your husband, lady. You're in trouble," Rafe mumbled, nuzzling his mouth into her hair. "Your hair always smells so good."

Cady sighed, her hands slipping around his middle.

"Cady? Rafe? Are you in there?" Professor Nesbitt called through the door. "Bruno Trabold is here and he says you should hurry."

Rafe lifted his face, red mottling his features. He stared at Cady for long moments, a muscle working in his jaw. Then his gaze lifted from her face and hardened before he turned toward the door, not releasing her as he spoke. "What the hell is he doing here? Never mind, Thomas, I'll be right there." He looked down again at Cady, a hard smile lifting one corner of his mouth. "Bruno seems to time his arrivals to interfere with us, wouldn't you agree?"

"I've always thought Bruno was a pain, not just this minute but ever since I've known him," Cady remarked, easing herself out of his arms and straightening her clothes.

"Especially when he knocked on my bedroom door that first time on Santo Tomas Island, right?" Rafe laughed as he watched the color run up her throat. He leaned down to give her a quick kiss. "I wanted to make love to you that day, Cady. I needed it so much, I thought I'd blow apart, but I also knew the first time should be when we were all alone." He pushed at the soft curve of hair that fell forward on her face. "Funny thing about you, lady. You never become angry when I touch your hair." He feathered her face with his lips. "There's another funny thing—I still want you as much as I did that day on Santo Tomas." He pushed back from her and went to the door, calling over his shoulder for her to hurry.

Cady felt as though someone had nailed her feet to the floor. Had Rafe said he loved her? Was that what he meant? If you wanted someone for a long time, wasn't that love? Oh, damn! She grabbed her handbag. If only she could be objective about Rafe. Maybe then she could sense more about his needs for her instead of having the feeling of being on another planet where he was concerned.

She ran down the stairs and came up short when she saw Bruno. "Where's Rafe?" she asked, assessing the other man warily.

"He's with your father." Bruno's smile was a mere lifting of the lips. His eyes kept the same arctic coldness as they roved over her body, his gaze insolent.

Her jaw rigid, she let her own eyes imitate his, trying to make her scrutiny of him the mirror image of his and hoping that the contempt she felt for him would be obvious in her face. "Well, Bruno, I don't know how I measure up with you, but you just don't make it on my tally sheet." She stepped closer to him and let her index finger just touch his abdomen. "You know, you really should do something about that potbelly. Suck it in or lose some weight. You might look better." Not allowing him time to answer, she scurried for the kitchen, feeling the heat in her cheeks. She leaned against the refrigerator door, taking deep breaths. She had never been so outspoken with Bruno before! First pouring her drink over him at the picnic and now insulting him! Was she going through some crazy change of life? Well, if she was, she liked it! She pulled herself up and took another deep breath. I don't have to take any guff from that mental midget, she told herself.

The kitchen door swung open. Rafe started to speak, then his eyes narrowed on her. "What happened? You look flushed. Are you all right? If this is going to make you ill, Cady, you don't have to do it." Rafe had had one hand in his trouser pocket in his usual stance, with his suit coat pushed back, but now he moved forward, concern on his face.

"No way are you going to take my speech from me." Cady could feel her jaw pushing out and her chin coming up. "At the moment I could wrestle a bear if I had to . . . but I'd rather not." She gave him a jaunty grin, then reached up and pressed his lips together, her touch feather light.

"Senators should not go around with their mouths open. It damages their credibility." She nibbled at his chin and then walked around him into the hall.

"Cady, come back here! Tell me what's going on! Cady?"

She found her father just closing the study door. She took his arm and squeezed it. "Come along, Professor Nesbitt, I'll escort you to the helicopter."

"You're looking pleased with yourself, young lady. What has put that cat-ate-the-puddin' look on your face?" her father quizzed in his mild way.

"I didn't rush my fence and I took the jump clean," Cady answered. As a young girl, she had learned to ride and jump at her father's urging. He loved the sport. Cady had learned to like horses, but she had never been much of an equestrienne, her riding proficient but not of a competitive class.

"I see. And would the plebian Mr. Trabold be at the root of this mild triumph?" The professor cleared his throat, his eyes shining with amusement.

"Yes, he would be, but I'm not going to tell you anything more," Cady lilted at him as he locked the front door. She sensed Rafe walking next to her toward the whirring blades of the helicopter, but she didn't look up.

During the hustle-bustle of the helicopter trip to the city and then the quick briefing with some of his aides, Rafe was kept too busy to talk with Cady. Then they left for the plane that was to take them to Monroe County.

Often during the short drive to the airport she felt Rafe's eyes on her, but she pretended to be engrossed in going over her speech, as she did during the plane ride. The strangest thing for Cady was that she felt no concern about the upcoming rally. Rather, she felt a sense of peace and confidence that she wouldn't let Rafe down.

People flocked around them the moment the plane landed at the county airport. Rafe's phenomenal memory enabled Cady to get through the name-recollection game that so many people played with elected officials. It seemed to her that at least fifty people asked her if she remembered them. She would nod and smile and almost always Rafe was there to supply her with the name just at the right time. The tight clasp of his hand was a comfort to her. More than once she saw someone glance at their entwined fingers, but when she tried to pull away, Rafe's clasp only tightened. More than once he leaned down to kiss her cheek or laugh at what she said to someone.

The ballroom of the hotel was filled to capacity, making Cady halt at the open double doors in momentary panic. For an instant she wanted to run away, but then she felt Rafe's warm palm at her back as people spotted them from their positions at the round luncheon tables. They all seemed to rise at once and begin applauding. Cady knew that most of these people were enthusiastic about Rafe's candidacy and members of his party, but that didn't stop the rush of good feeling that coursed through her as the applause swelled and there were shouts of "Rafe, Rafe." Her mouth dropped open when she heard people call "Cady, Cady."

She listened as Rafe gave a satisfied laugh at her side and then hugged her arm close to his body. "They love you, darling, and I don't blame them."

She looked up at him, feeling a flush of pleasure at his words, but he was looking around at the crowd, smiling and waving.

The luncheon was the usual pasteboard fare served at political gatherings, but to Cady it tasted like a gourmet delight because she was squeezed close to Rafe on the dais with the other dignitaries. He spoke to everyone near them and smiled often at the people sitting at the round tables in front of the raised platform. Yet it seemed to Cady that whenever Rafe looked past her to speak, he took the opportunity of placing his arm around her shoulder. When he looked the other way, his hand would grasp hers under the table. She beamed down at her father, who was seated at a table in her line of vision. She was happy. Being with Rafe gave her a special feeling.

Her sense of well-being lasted through the chicken salad and limp spinach vinaigrette. As the time ap-

proached for her to speak, the coffee began to turn acid
in her stomach. The familiar flutterings in her abdomen
that she'd had to fight since grade school whenever she
was called on to recite or answer a question seemed to
gather momentum. When the chairman of the fund raiser
stood to give the opening remarks, Cady switched from
coffee to ice water, hoping that her insides would steady.
She took deep breaths as the man began his introduction
of Rafe, who would in turn introduce her.

"Cady, I'm very proud to be your husband, and if you
rose to your feet and lost your lunch on the mayor's
head, I would still be very proud of you," Rafe whispered, his breath tickling her ear. He planted a light kiss
on her cheekbone.

Cady hiccupped a laugh, then put her hand over her
mouth, gazing reproachfully at her husband as she tried
to stifle her mirth at the picture his words had conjured
up. He had that puckish look on his face that told Cady
he was laughing at her.

Before she could reply, his name was mentioned and
the applause rose like a wave.

With a casual tug at his tie, he bent to kiss her parted
lips, the momentary intimacy he gave the caress surprising her. Mischief glittered in his eyes as he stepped
toward the microphone. Her butterflies evaporated. Her
fingers unclenched.

Rafe's speech was pungent and witty. He didn't take
personal swipes at his opponent. Rather, he stressed what
had been achieved under his own leadership in the Senate
and the crippling effects his opponent's economic poli-
cies would have on the state.

Cady had heard her husband speak many times, but
the electric effect he had on audiences never ceased to
amaze her. Though he had always lived in the lap of
luxury, his political aspirations included reforms for the
poor and underprivileged and plans to reinforce the working structure for the middle class. Cady had lost none of
the dedication toward Rafe's goals that she had felt as a
college sophomore. As she listened to him outline his

proposed programs, she was more and more convinced of his caring attitude toward his job.

When he switched to talk of her and all the benefits that had accrued to him by being married to such an able woman, Cady couldn't help the rush of blood to her face. He praised the work she had done while he lay incapacitated, outlining her accomplishments to the assembled people. He concluded, "I'm proud to introduce my wife to you. Ladies and gentlemen, Cady Densmore. Come here, darling."

Cady wasn't sure anyone else had heard his last words because the applause was so loud, but they put steel in her spine. She walked to the mike, accepted his kiss, then turned to smile at the audience as he sat down, waiting for silence.

Rafe rose once again and walked to the mike, adjusting it downward. "Sometimes I forget how tiny she is," he mumbled to the audience, making them laugh.

Cady laughed with them, then began to speak. She told of the the measures she had fought for while Rafe was ill, the struggles she'd had. When she was almost through with her prepared text, she sensed that the audience was with her. It gave her a sense of power. When she might have drawn to a close, she pushed her papers aside and looked out at the crowd. She cleared her throat. "I've told you about our goals and what we've done. I know that you are aware, as well, of all my husband went through while he was trapped in the grip of paralysis." She swallowed around the sudden lump in her throat. "But none of you was there to see this vibrant man totally still except for his eyes—eyes that mirrored his agony yet also showed the indomitable will that wouldn't allow him to surrender or die."

There wasn't a sound in the cavernous room; not even a swallow. Everyone was frozen, looking at her.

"There were times when I wanted to give up, but the fire in his eyes wouldn't let me," Cady continued, her voice hoarse. "That's why I know Rafe Densmore will never surrender his integrity or his beliefs in this state.

He's the strongest man I know, and he will fight for us and our concerns. Thank you."

There was total silence as Cady turned away from the mike. Her eyes sought and found her husband's. His face was expressionless. He didn't even rise to hold out her chair. The scrape of the legs of her chair hitting his was like a signal in the stillness.

There was a roar of applause as chairs were pushed back and people surged to their feet. They shouted, "Rafe, Rafe," and "That-a girl, Cady."

When the clapping showed no signs of letting up, Rafe rose, bringing Cady with him, holding her close to his side as he waved to the emotion-filled crowd.

When they were finally able to push their way through the people, and Cady had signed numerous programs and Rafe had done the same, they entered the limousine that would take them to the airport.

"That was a good touch, Cady," Bruno offered dryly. "Always inject a little tearjerker. Gets 'em every time." He smirked at a pale-faced Cady from his place on the jump seat in the limousine.

Rafe glowered at him. "Bruno, I think it would be better for you to work with my father from now on. Don't bother coming on the campaign. I won't need you."

"Hey, Rafe, Emmett won't like that," Bruno blustered, his fingers snapping in half the cigar he was about to light.

"Tough," Rafe responded, his voice flat. "Make sure you're on the flight back to Washington tonight. I'm putting out the word that you won't be on the campaign any longer. If you don't take the flight tonight, you can walk." Rafe leaned across Cady and asked her father if he would like a drink before pushing the switch that opened the built-in bar.

Rafe was laughing at the professor's look of amazement and didn't see the nasty glance Bruno gave him. Cady saw it and shivered. When Bruno turned that same gaze on her, it took all her courage to face him rather than turn way. Bruno Trabold was Rafe's enemy. Cady had never been more sure of anything in her life.

She was glad when Bruno left them as soon as they arrived at the county airport. She assured her father that she and Rafe would be back at their home in Tompkins County in upstate New York in a day or so. "Rafe has another rally to attend in the area, then we'll be going to New York City for a couple of days, but we'll come home first."

"That was a fine speech, Cady," her father told her, his voice mild. "You're a fighter, daughter, just like your mother was." He looked past her at Rafe, who was talking with some of his aides and waiting patiently for Cady to make her good-byes to her father. "I saw a side of Rafe I've never seen before today, Cady. I realized that he is and always has been a lonely person, man and boy. I watched the way he looked at you when you discussed him during your speech. His eyes had the hungry, deprived look of the very lonely."

Cady would have scoffed, laughed even, at the preposterous notion that Rafe of the large family, the huge circle of friends, could be lonely. She looked at her father's serious, almost grim look and did neither. "Father, you're wrong, I'm sure of it. Rafe is one of the most gregarious men I've ever known. People are naturally drawn to him."

"I suppose you're right. You should know your own husband," Professor Nesbitt declared woodenly, lifting his grip and heading toward the small private plane that would take him to the airport at Ithaca. A car would be waiting there to take him to his home.

Cady couldn't get her father's words out of her head on the return car trip to the hotel where they would stay overnight. Rafe was busy talking to an aide now and then, but she felt his intent stare.

What had Trock said to her while they were walking in the rose garden at the Highlands? That so often Rafe was alone, that his family was very offhand in coming to see him, that there were long hours when he was by himself. Before Cady could consider any more of the questions plaguing her, they were drawing up in front of the hotel and a coterie of media people was lining the sidewalk.

On entering the hotel lobby they were again besieged by well-wishers and autograph seekers. Cady watched, smiling, as her husband fielded questions and signed numerous pieces of paper or copies of the article that he had written for *Day Magazine*.

Cady didn't feel the tug on her arm at first. When she turned around, she looked straight into the eyes of a woman who was a little taller than herself, but older and more careworn. The stranger's brown hair was streaked with gray, the eyes tired but with an innate warmth. Cady smiled and inclined her head, thinking the woman wanted an autograph.

"Mrs. Densmore, I know you're a busy woman, but I just have to talk to you. I read the writeup of your opinion of dog fighting. Did you mean it? Are you against the destruction of the bull terrier through illegal fighting?"

Cady frowned at the intense woman, noting how she twisted her hands together. "Yes, I'm very much against pit fighting."

The woman looked nervously at the crowd of people around her. "I don't like talking here, but I have to speak with you."

Cady looked at Rafe, who was conversing in an absorbed way with a man who looked like a student. Then she turned to an aide, touching his arm. "Would you tell the senator that I've gone upstairs, please?"

The man nodded and smiled, throwing a quick glance at the harried woman at Cady's side.

Cady led the woman to the elevator and pushed the button for their floor. Neither one spoke until the elevator stopped and they had traversed the hall leading to the suite. Cady ushered the woman inside and pointed to a sofa in the all-white window-walled room. Cady rang for coffee, then joined the woman on the couch. "Now, Mrs. . . ."

"My name is Proctor, Ruth Proctor, and I'm a widow." The woman crossed, then uncrossed her legs, her gaze sliding away from Cady's. "My husband was a wonderful man, Mrs. Densmore, but when he was killed in an industrial accident, I found myself in the position of having to get a job after years of being a housewife. Luckily I found a job with our local police department and can even walk to work. I have one son who has been no trouble to me, but I have a brother-in-law who was nothing but trouble to both my husband and myself.

"I told him to stay away from my son and me, and he did until about two months ago. Then he came to the house apologizing for being a hindrance to us, and by way of making it up he said he wanted to present our son with a dog, a genuine pit terrier with papers and everything. At first I thought a dog would be too much work, but Max—that's the dog's name—turned out to be a wonderful companion for my son and a good watch-dog. He's very smart and clean. Both Jerry, my son, and I love Max.

"About a month ago my brother-in-law, Ted, came to the house and said he wanted to take Max overnight because he was keeping some valuables in the house. I didn't want the dog to go, but I didn't feel that I could refuse because Ted had given us the dog. When Max was returned to us on Sunday, he was badly marked with some really deep slashes. Ted said that someone had tried to break into his house. I didn't believe him because Ted always lies, but I didn't say anything. Twice more he borrowed the dog. This past time he didn't return him." Ruth Proctor sobbed. "I think Max is dead. Jerry wants me to tell the police, but I don't want to get my brother-in-law in trouble if he isn't breaking the law. He has a record, you see. I just don't know what to do." She wiped her eyes with a crumpled tissue. "Mrs. Densmore, my son is in misery."

"Where does your brother-in-law live, Ruth? I'll go with you tomorrow and we'll ask him where the dog is." Cady knew she was sticking her neck way out and that Rafe would be angry with her, but at the moment all she could see was a young boy's face, hurt and miserable without his dog.

She made up her mind that she would tell Rafe before she accompanied Mrs. Proctor, and she arranged to meet the woman the next day. But somehow there never seemed to be an opportune moment to talk with him.

That evening she and Rafe attended a formal fund raiser. They were both so tired when they returned home that they fell into bed. The next morning Cady found a note from Rafe telling her that he had let her sleep while he went to a meeting at campaign headquarters. Cady left a note telling Rafe where she was going and why. Then she called down to the desk and ordered a rented car. As an added precaution she left the address where she and Ruth Proctor hoped to find the dog.

When she picked up Ruth Proctor, the woman was nervous, but Cady felt confident that she was doing something that would not shame her husband and at the same time would help a young boy.

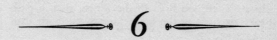

6

"MY BROTHER-IN-LAW IS a bully, Mrs. Densmore, but he doesn't want trouble with the law. He went to prison a few years back and it almost killed him." Ruth Proctor spoke in a rather shaken voice as she and Cady sat in the parked car on a seedy residential street. "That house used to belong to my mother-in-law, and when she owned it this street was beautifully kept up. Her house looked the best of them." She shrugged. "Streets change. Sometimes the people that move in don't care about the property. That's what happened to this street. My husband was sure that Ted would change if we let him have his mother's house. He didn't." Ruth Proctor stopped speaking in the nervous way she had when a car came down the street and several men alighted from the vehicle. They went around the garage of the house toward the back. "There's an old barn out in back," Ruth whispered. "The property stretches all the way to the next street. Mrs. Densmore, I've changed my mind. I don't think it would be a good idea to go in there. We should call the police.

Even if we go in the back way..." Her voice trailed off.

Cady nodded. "Right, but we can't leave to call them. Let's take a look at the barn and see if they have pit dogs there. If they do, we'll go into your brother-in-law's house and call the police."

Ruth Proctor looked horrified. "What if someone sees us?"

"Didn't you say that you knew a way onto the property that wasn't used very often?" Cady asked the skeptical woman. "If we use that, no one will see us."

"Ye-es, through old Mr. Schuler's orchard. Gerald, my husband, and I used to go there when we wanted to be alone. There's a hole in the fence, then a path that will take us right to the back door of the barn. But that was years ago..."

"We'll try that. Maybe we'll find Max in the barn."

Ruth pressed her lips together and nodded.

They turned the car around and went down another street that had a cement and coal company on it and a large empty lot. Ruth Proctor pointed to a narrow dirt drive that led through the vacant lot. Cady drove until she came to a high mesh fence.

It took a few minutes to find the break in the fence. Cady blessed the jeans she was wearing as the torn wire, then the brambles and burrs along the path, pulled at her. The orchard was overgrown with weeds, but there were some nice-size apples on the trees.

The women looked at each other, then ran the short distance from the orchard to the barn.

Cady tried the door. It stuck, then opened partially. She decided not to try to force a larger opening in case it would make a sound. She listened for a moment, with Ruth Proctor pressed at her back. She could hear the sounds of men laughing, followed by a brief silence. One man spoke. Then there was an awful din of growling, snarling, tearing, pain-filled shrieks. Cady could feel her stomach rise into her throat as she imagined the agony of the yowling animals. She turned to face Ruth and whispered close to her ear, "Go to the house. Call the police. Those dogs are being killed. Hurry!"

Ruth Proctor gave a quick nod and scurried away.

Cady squeezed through the narrow opening, snagging her long-sleeved pullover on the splintered wood. Her nostrils distended, assaulted by the smells of blood and excrement. She stood still in the murky area, adjusting her eyes to the dimness. She saw three dogs in pens, all of them scarred, one lying on its side, bleeding from several gashes, its breathing harsh. At first none of them moved when they saw her. Then the dog nearest to her—the biggest one—rose to his feet and leaned against the mesh, his short tail waving slowly back and forth, a low sound emanating from his throat.

"Easy, boy. I'm not going to hurt you," Cady said softly. She looked into those sad eyes again, the proud white snout marred by a jagged scar not yet healed. "In fact," she whispered, feeling anger rise in her, "I'm going to free you."

The cage wasn't locked, but she tried to be careful lest she make a noise. She released the three dogs, but only the big one followed her as she made her way toward the front of the barn where the shouting of the men and the snarling and growling of the dogs was becoming more frenzied. She pushed back a tattered curtain and saw the men and the pit terriers. All seemed to be foaming from the mouth. Blood was everywhere.

One of the dogs was flagging and the men were yelling, "Kill, Blanco, kill!"

Horror held Cady for tense moments; then she looked around for some way to stop the fight. She saw a large hose of the type used by firefighters coiled on the floor just in front of her. The hose was attached to a huge spigot, which Cady surmised acted as the shutoff valve. Next to the spigot a key dangled from a nail on the wall—doubtless the key to the spigot. Without a second thought Cady reached for the key and inserted it, turning it easily. She felt the rush of water at her feet and strained to aim and hold the nozzle of the hose. A few of the spectators were turning her way, but it seemed to Cady they were looking in slow motion as the water erupted from the nozzle. She felt as though she were on the back of a wild steer. She aimed the hose into the crowd, but it had a life of its own and sprayed everywhere. She closed her eyes and hung on to the exploding snake in her hand, knowing she couldn't hold it long because the power was too much for her. She felt the dog at the back of her legs, but she could hear nothing except the roars of the men and the pulsating bellow of the water.

Next thing she knew she was on the ground next to the dog, lying in odorous mud, an angry, very wet man standing above her with the key in his hand. Cady gave a quick glance toward the arena where the dogs had been fighting. Both animals were lying on their sides, tongues lolling, bodies heaving as they fought for air. Fresh blood oozed from several deep cuts.

"Who the hell are you? And what the hell are you doing in my barn?" The man, whom Cady assumed was Ted Proctor, brandished the key like a weapon.

Cady swallowed once, deciding to brazen it out, hoping that Ruth had gotten to a phone. "That's my dog in there. It was stolen from me." She looked back at the white dog behind her, which was pressed close to her back. The terrier wasn't looking at her; he was looking up at the man. "And this is my dog as well. See, he knows me," Cady lied. "The police have been called and you're going to be arrested." Cady tried to sit erect in the goo but only succeeded in covering herself more completely with mud. The white dog was getting browner.

One of the other men was standing nearby and heard the conversation. He was soaked and leaning forward, trying to shake some of the excess water from his body. "Damn it, Ted, I don't want no trouble with the cops. And you didn't say nothin' about no dames, either. I'm gettin' outta here. Otis, you comin' with me?"

"Yeah, Harry, I'm comin'. Wait till I pour the water outta my wallet. I got a good mind to punch that broad." The scowling Otis squished toward Cady, his feet making a sucking sound as he tried to make his way through the mud.

"Just hold it right there, buddy. You're not punching anyone." Rafe's voice was harsh, his body thrusting forward as he moved in from the front door of the barn.

Cady recognized the two men just behind him as campaign aides. She stared goggle-eyed at her husband. He was all denim-clad menace, his eyes a leaping green fire. This must be the look that his political foes described as Rafe's street-fighter stare, Cady mused, unable to look away from the man she loved. He must have read her note, she thought. How fast he'd gotten here! Oh, Lord, Rafe, please be careful.

"What the hell is going on here, Ted?" another man whined. "I don't like all these people. You said this was going to be private, just a few friends. I don't like it."

"Shut up, Frankie," Ted muttered. "They got no right on my property."

Cady felt immobilized as she continued to watch Rafe. The glitter in his eye held hard amusement. He was poised on the balls of his feet, a slight upward curve to his lips. She wanted to speak to him, but the words stuck in her throat.

"If this is your broad, take her and get outta here while you can still walk." Ted brandished the key in his hand, waving it toward Cady's head.

Rafe's face seemed to take on a yellow cast as he looked from the key to Cady. "Cady, come here." His voice was hoarse.

Cady struggled to rise, slipping in the stickiness. "We have to get Max, too, Rafe," she panted, almost erect.

"Wait a minute here." Ted hooked the key around Cady's arm, jerking her back into the mud. "What's this about—" he started to ask.

With an angry snarl Rafe launched himself through the air at Ted, who was looking down at Cady.

As Ted looked up, hearing the threatening rage in Rafe's yell, he attempted to bring the steel key up to protect himself.

Cady threw herself upward, latching onto Ted's arm so that he couldn't bring the key into position.

Ted swore. The dog behind Cady whined, then growled. The other men began shouting and milling about. Rafe hit Ted chest high, flinging him into the mud alongside Cady.

Cady was almost blinded by the mud, but when she saw the man called Frankie try to come to Ted's aid, she picked up a handful of mud and threw it straight into his face and yelled, "Get him, boy," to the dog.

"You lousy bitch," Frankie squealed, then he howled as the bull terrier landed on him with a ferocious snarl.

There was no way to tell friend from foe when the police whistle sounded. Ruth Proctor was screaming, "Mrs. Densmore, Mrs. Densmore, where are you? Oh, help, help, someone, we have to find Mrs. Densmore." Her voice was shrill and bordering on hysteria. Cady knew that even if she screamed back, the other woman might not hear her. The din was ear shattering.

Cady was struggling to her feet when she saw Frankie tear himself away from the dog and try to make a break for the back door. Without thinking Cady launched herself at his back, hearing her husband's voice in her ears.

"Cady—don't—uuuuuhhh!" The breath left Rafe's lungs as he was pummeled backward.

Cady looked over her shoulder at Rafe as she lay astride Frankie's back. The bull terrier had now positioned himself at Frankie's head, his growls and snapping jaws keeping the prone Frankie immobile.

"Damn it, lady, get offa me. Aaagh, I got mud in my mouth . . ."

A policeman leaned down and lifted Cady from Frankie's back. "Here you are, ma'am. Stay right here and let me take care of this fellow for you. Easy, now, dog. Take it easy." Though the policeman spoke in soft tones, his face had a don't-mess-with-me look as he dragged Frankie to his feet.

Before long the police had restored order, and Ted

and two of his friends were being led in handcuffs to police cars.

Cady patted the dog whose head was pressed against her leg and tried to wave to Ruth Proctor as the noise lessened gradually.

Finally Rafe managed to introduce himself to the police. As Rafe helped her to her feet, Cady could see the incredulous looks on the faces of the two officers, but she was too busy trying to reassure the crying Ruth Proctor to say anything. Rafe could handle it.

As the police led some of the men away, Cady told them she wanted to speak to Ted. "Where's Max?" she confronted him. "Have you killed him?"

"Naw, don't be stupid," Ted rasped, then stepped closer to the policeman as Rafe made for him again.

"Watch your mouth when you speak to my wife," Rafe ordered in a menacing tone. "Now where's this Max?"

Before Ted could respond, Ruth Proctor let out a groan and knelt beside one of the dogs, cradling the dirty, bloodstained animal to her.

"Hey, Ruth, for God's sake be proud of him. He's the best fighter I ever had," Ted asserted. Ruth laid the dog's head on her jacket, then rose to her feet, walking toward her brother-in-law.

"Don't you ever come near me or Jerry again, Ted Proctor." She lifted her arm and smacked him full force in the face, rocking him back on his heels. "And don't you ever come near my dog again, either."

"Good for you, Ruth," Cady applauded as the officers led Ted away.

Before long Rafe and his aides had arranged with the police for the care of the dogs and assured Ruth Proctor that Max would be taken to the best veterinarian possible. Since there were no known owners for the other dogs, the police told Rafe they would contact the SPCA.

Cady took hold of Rafe's arm as they walked to the car. "You shouldn't have done that—fought that man,

I mean," she whispered, swallowing. "Your spine . . . your operation . . ." She bit down on her lip. "I didn't think there would be any fighting."

Rafe leaned down to kiss her. "I've had tougher workouts with the twins. Don't worry." He looked past her at the dog Cady had insisted that she would keep, watching as the animal followed her docilely into the taxi. "What are you going to do with him, Cady?" Rafe asked as he tried to wipe some of the caking mud from her face. "I hope you know we'll have to face a barrage of reporters when we return to the hotel. You're not looking your best, Mrs. Densmore." He chuckled.

"You don't look that good yourself, Senator." Cady stilled his hand on her face. "Will this hurt your campaign, Rafe? Will it damage you in any way?"

"I doubt it—might even help. In the past there have been exposés about illegal dogfights in this city and people have been very angry about it. Don't worry, love; I'm not."

"Then to answer your question about the dog, I'm going to keep him. If a real owner is found, I'll return him, of course, but the police seemed to think the animals could have been stolen when they were pups or even purchased by some of the men who were arrested. The officers didn't think any of the men would admit to ownership because of legal repercussions related to dogfighting." Cady took a breath and smiled at the dog that sat on the floor of the car, looking up at her. "I'm going to call him Hobo."

The trip back to the hotel seemed to take mere minutes. When she saw the battery of cameras, Cady was glad the overwrought Ruth Proctor had been taken home by the police. She blinked at the flash of lights as the cameramen moved in.

Rafe promised to answer all their questions if they would just give him and his wife a chance to wash and change clothes. A press conference was hurriedly called by Rafe's aide, and all at once Cady had another schedule to meet.

* * *

Cady was sure she would never be able to get used to the blinding effect of the television lights. She was in awe of the panache with which her husband handled the press conference. Suddenly Cady realized that all eyes were on her. Since she had been concentrating on Rafe, she hadn't heard the question. Her eyes beseeched Rafe, and he repeated the question in low tones, calming her at once.

"How did I find out about this? Good question. There are many public spirited citizens who come forth with information, especially to my husband. They know that Rafe is a man of honor—"

"Yes, Mrs. Densmore, we are all aware of the opinion you have of your husband," a woman with a ginger-color friz of hair stated, making the others laugh, including Rafe. "But the woman came to *you*. Doesn't that make you a potent figure in your husband's campaign and in his political life?"

"I'd like to answer that, Cady, if you don't mind," Rafe interjected, giving her a reassuring smile. Then he looked directly into one of the television cameras. "My wife, Cady Densmore, is the most potent factor in my political life as well as my private life. Cady's integrity and her innate dignity are prime forces in all I do. I'm very proud of her."

Cady didn't hear much more of the conference. She was too wrapped up in Rafe's glowing words of praise for her. She hugged them and turned them over in her mind, feeling as gleeful as a child at Christmas. Rafe cared for her. She would make that caring grow into love.

Rafe finished the conference by vowing that he intended to do all he could to eradicate various types of injustice and to protect the vulnerable—whether they were the elderly, children, or animals—from victimization.

Cady applauded along with everyone else, relieved that he looked so fit.

Back in their suite, she thought that Rafe would want to rest awhile, but to her surprise he followed her into her room.

"We both need a rest after that wild time today, but I'd like to speak to you, Cady. So if you don't mind, I'll lie down on your bed." He yawned as he yanked the tie from around his neck. "I'm always glad when a campaign is over. Then I can go back to wearing sport shirts." He sighed and threw himself backward on the king-size bed, waving his hand at her to come join him.

When she sat down, he reached up and began lifting the sweater over her head and unzipping her skirt. "You can't be relaxed wrapped up in all that clothing. Shall I take off your panty hose?" Rafe laughed when she reddened and said that she could do it. He pulled her under the quilted cover and hugged her close to his body. "Now, as for putting yourself in danger as you did this morning—don't ever do that again. I almost had a heart attack when I saw that creep Ted Proctor standing over you. Cady, you know I want your help in everything, but I don't want you in danger. Clear?"

"Clear... but, Rafe, I couldn't refuse Ruth Proctor. She's such a nice woman, and life hasn't been easy for her."

"I could tell that, angel. That's why I want to arrange for a college scholarship for her boy Jerry when he comes of age. I understand from his mother that he's very interested in engineering, so if he still feels that way when he finishes high school, the money will be there for Clarkson or any of the other good engineering schools in this state."

"Oh, Rafe..." Cady could feel her eyes filling with tears as she turned toward him on the bed. "You're such a good man."

"Good enough for you to keep, my love?" Rafe quizzed her, his voice gruff.

"Rafe, you're so foolish. Of course I want to keep you. Didn't I show you that all the months you were so ill?" Cady let her fingers trace his chin line, liking the roughness of his stubbled skin.

"I don't want your pity, Cady. I want more," he mumbled, his face in her hair.

"How could you have more? You have all of me now." She felt as daring as if she had just disclosed high-level state secrets.

"Have I? That's what I want, Cady—all of you, all the time. I can't settle for less. The wanting is stronger every day, my love."

"Mine, too," Cady breathed, turning on her side to face him on the pillow, mouth to mouth with him, skin to skin.

"Cady, darling, you're so warm. You make me feel that I'll never be cold again as long as I have you near me." Rafe's breathing was ragged on her face.

Cady could see the streaks of color run up his neck as his muscles grew taut with need. She could feel her own shivering response as he began the familiar exploration of her body.

"Cady, darling, I *need* this so. I want it so," he mumbled, letting his mouth rove her form, his tongue a hot pleasure that fired her feeling for him.

His hands cupped her breasts, his thumbs lifting to tease her hardening nipples even as his lips moved down her body. His hoarse mutterings of satisfaction increased as his mouth traced a path down her abdomen to her thighs.

Her body quivered in involuntary reaction to the joy he was giving her, arching toward him like a drawn bow. "Rafe...I...can't believe my feelings," she groaned, her hands digging into him to pull him even closer.

He gave a husky laugh and tightened his hold on her, but when he leaned back to say something to her, Cady wouldn't release him, nibbling at his chin.

The heat built in both of them to an intolerable pressure. When Cady thought surely she would fly apart, they climaxed together. She felt as if the planet had separated, all the stars in the galaxy had fallen earthward, and only she and Rafe were floating out there in space. They descended slowly back to earth, still clinging to each other.

"Rafe," Cady mumbled from the tight haven of his arms. "It's more beautiful than ever to me. Is it to you?"

He chuckled into her hair. "Cady, love, it's you. You keep getting more beautiful." He leaned back from her, letting one finger lift her chin so he could look at her. "When I was in the nursing home, I used to look at you and weep inside, knowing that I could never love you again. That was sheer agony for me. I wanted you so much and couldn't reach out and touch you. When you would lean over and kiss my forehead, I wanted to yell at you to kiss my lips so I could feel your mouth—if only for a moment. My eyes could see you lift my hand and put your lips to it, but I couldn't feel you do it and it tore me apart." Rafe's voice had the sound of ripping cloth as he described his feelings.

"Oh, Rafe, I hated it when you were paralyzed. I could feel how you hated it, too. That's why I went ahead with the operation." She enclosed his head with her arms, striving to comfort him, wanting him to forget those awful days when he was a prisoner of his own body.

"If you keep stroking me like that, Cady love, we'll never leave this bed." When Rafe lifted his head, she saw he had that elfin look on his face, the laughter in his eyes not masking the heat that glittered there.

"I remember on our honeymoon we did that. Stayed in bed all day, I mean." Cady felt out of breath as she looked at her husband. "I don't suppose you could tell Ray that we're too tired to join him for..." Cady felt herself lifted and put aside as Rafe reached for the phone.

In a few terse words Rafe was through and turning to reach for her again. "So much for that. Now where were we?"

Cady felt balloon-light as her husband began to caress her again. Rafe was hers, if only for a short while. The campaign would take him again and there would be other things to pull him from her side when they returned to Washington, but for now he was hers.

The next day they returned to their lakefront home and prepared for the clambake they were giving for some people who, Rafe informed her, were fence-sitters in the campaign.

When the guests began arriving in the early afternoon, Cady was once more gratified by the number of people who approached her and mentioned her work on the Hill.

"You're an asset to Rafe, daughter." Her father smiled down at her after overhearing some of the guests sing his daughter's praises. "I think Rafe agrees with me." Professor Nesbitt strolled with Cady around the grounds while she stopped and spoke to people or just smiled and nodded.

"I like to think that I'm a help to Rafe," she said, waving to some children who were riding horseback down the cliff path. She took her father's arm and squeezed it, feeling a sense of deep happiness. "Rafe looks wonderful, doesn't he?"

Her father followed her gaze, watching Rafe laughing with some men, a stein of beer in one hand, the other hand in its characteristic position on his hip. As though he felt their gaze, Rafe turned, fixing his eyes on them, then smiling, his lips pursing in a kiss as he looked at Cady.

"He's never looked better." The professor tamped his pipe on his open hand, his forehead creasing as he watched a man approach them. "Cady, is that...?" He squinted.

Cady looked in the direction her father was staring and started. The medium-tall man with the thinning sandy hair and rather dissipated air was familiar. How could she ever have thought Todd Leacock attractive! she mused as he came closer. More to the point, what was he doing at Rafe's fund-raising clambake? Cady racked her brain as she tried to remember if Todd had ever talked of having political leanings. She could not recall that he had. She shrugged inwardly. Perhaps he had decided to get more involved in politics.

She couldn't help thinking how poorly he compared to her husband. Like a good politician's wife, she summoned up a smile, even though she wasn't glad to see him.

"Hello, Cady. Professor Nesbitt." Todd's smile had the assurance of someone who assumed he would be welcome.

Cady stared at him—his receding hairline, his beginning paunch—and her smile widened. "Todd Leacock. How are you? I had forgotten that you live near us in Seneca County." She kept her smile as natural as she could, even though she was laughing inside at the young and foolish eighteen-year-old who had thought herself in love with him. Still, Todd had served one purpose. If she hadn't been upset and gone to her room, Rafe would never have come there to soothe her. Just thinking that made her smile more genuine and her handshake more enthusiastic. She was a little puzzled by the smug look that came over Todd's face before he turned to greet her father.

Cady remembered that the professor had never liked Todd much, so she wasn't surprised when he excused himself and wandered off toward the group surrounding Rafe.

"Well, Cady, tell me about yourself." Todd put his arm around her waist.

At once Cady moved away, annoyed. "I'm fine. Very happily married to Rafe, as you can see. How are you?"

"I'm very happily divorced," he said ironically, as if mocking her. "For a while I worked for a camera supply outfit in the city. Then I opened my own camera shop. I photograph weddings and other events, sell equipment to photo buffs. It's a pretty good business. I like being my own boss." He looked at her for long moments. "I did some work for some associates of your husband when he campaigned in Rochester. I enjoyed that."

"Sounds good," Cady replied, struggling not to yawn. It had been a long day.

"I'd like to take some pictures of you, Cady." Todd shifted the camera from his shoulder.

She blinked. "Why?"

He shrugged. "Oh, sometimes I write articles for the Sunday supplements, and I think I could sell pictures of you to them. You know, senator's wife, that sort of thing." Todd's smile had a stale charm, Cady thought.

"All right, but I think the papers and periodicals already have plenty of pictures of me." Smiling into the camera, she looked up, then away. She was rather baffled when Todd went into a kneeling position on the ground and clicked his camera up at her. After several such shots she called a halt.

"Just a couple more, Cady. There . . ."

"No more, Todd. You must have thirty shots of me. No magazine will buy all those." She smiled at him mechanically and began walking away. "I really do have to circulate."

"I'll walk with you." He seemed impervious to any hint.

For the next hour Todd remained as if glued to her side, and Cady was very aware that he was still shooting pictures of her.

She could feel her irritation with him growing. All at once, when she had just about had enough, he seemed to disappear. Cady heaved a sigh of relief, because she had been on the point of telling him to get lost no matter what people might think of her. Todd Leacock was a pest!

The clambake was a success, but by the time everyone was leaving, Cady was exhausted. She looked for Rafe and her father and found them saying good-bye to friends on the front lawn. When the last car finally left, Cady tried unsuccessfully to persuade her father to stay for a snack. He had a class in the morning and was eager to get home.

Cady noticed Rafe's silence as they walked around the yard, picking up the trash in a desultory fashion. Tomorrow their handyman, Sid Gresham, would tidy the place in earnest. "Is something wrong, Rafe?"

"Why didn't you tell me that you had invited your old boyfriend to the clambake?" Rafe crumpled a foam cup in his hand before tossing it into the plastic-lined trash barrel.

"Because I didn't invite him! He used to live near here in Seneca County, but he lives in Rochester now." She shrugged, emptying an ashtray. "I guess he was visiting his folks for the weekend. Who cares?"

"You don't? Thomas reminded me that he was the one you were going with when I met you." Rafe turned to look at her, a muscle jumping in his cheek.

"Yes, I couldn't help thinking that was the one good thing Todd did."

Rafe's jaw worked as though it had a rusty hinge. "And what might that be?"

"If he hadn't shocked the daylights out of me by being in bed with Marina, I might not have come home when I did. Then a certain congressman might not have come up to my room." Cady smiled at him.

"I'll send him a CandyGram." Rafe's voice was still hard, but there was a flicker of blue heat in his eyes.

"Could that be construed as a bribe, Senator?" Cady felt her pulse jump out of rhythm as Rafe laced his fingers through hers.

"A payoff, I think," Rafe muttered, his hand still holding hers as he went behind her to press her closer to him. "Maybe we should clean up the bedroom now. No doubt it's a mess."

"No one was in there," Cady muttered into his neck.

"Let's check." He leaned back from her, his eyes lasering her. "Why aren't you angry with me for being such a jealous jackass?"

Cady lifted her free hand and touched his jaw. "I'm waiting until you're three kinds of jackass. Then I'll get mad at you."

"Long-suffering little thing, aren't you?" His hand slipped under her breast, squeezing in gentle motion.

"A true martyr," Cady gasped, her body yielding to him. "Senator, I don't think we should shock the neighbors, in case anyone should wander by."

"True." He turned her body but didn't allow her to move away from him. His arm tightened around her waist, he began leading her back to the house. "Election Day is almost on us. Feel the bite in the air. Still, we've had a beautiful autumn so far." He stopped her for a moment, lifting her chin so that he could watch her. "Whether I win or lose, we'll have to leave for Washington right after the election."

"You'll win. I know it." Cady wrapped her arms around his middle, her cheek pressed to his. She felt his lips on her hair.

"What I'm trying to say, wife of mine, is that we'll have precious little time alone back in Washington, so let's not waste the hours we have now." Rafe grinned at her. "How would you like to spend the next three days in bed with your husband?"

"Oh, shucks. I thought you were going to offer me Burt Reynolds." Cady chuckled and pushed against his chest.

Off-balance for a moment, Rafe wasn't able to stop her when she broke into a run. "Games, is it? Fine with me."

Cady was running as fast as she could, sure that she could beat Rafe to the house, when she felt something catch her around the waist. She was laughing so hard she couldn't even struggle when Rafe pulled her down on top of him. "How did you catch me? You're in better shape than you should be." Cady scowled down at him as he lay beneath her. They were in a brushy declivity, hidden from the house and the lake but not far from the cliff overlooking the water.

"Make love to me, Cady." Rafe's voice was hoarse.

"We can't—not here. You'll catch cold."

"We're hidden from the wind here and the sun is

warm . . . so is the ground," Rafe muttered, loosening her sweater and lifting it so he might caress her breasts with his lips. "Did I ever tell you that I love your breasts?"

"You may have mentioned it." Cady snuggled closer, loving the crisp softness of his bare chest against her.

Rafe sheltered her with his body when her clothes were removed. Cady felt safe and protected. Their hands on each other were sure yet hesitant as they both strove to control their own feelings and give the other satisfaction. Heat burned through the control like a blast furnace gone mad.

Cady felt wild, protective, loving, giving, wanting. Rafe's skin was as precious as platinum, and when it touched her it turned her to gold. They were alone in the inferno, cool in the middle of a fiery eye, serene in their love, calm in the center of the storm.

7

RAFE WAS REELECTED! The celebration had a Mardi Gras flavor, delighting Cady. Rafe had deserved to win. He was the best man for New York. Cady knew that and was happy when other people said the same thing.

When they returned to Washington, Rafe's staff was elated and gave a small party to welcome him back.

The weeks after their return were busy ones for both of them, but Rafe and Cady tried to make time for each other every day. Cady felt exhilarated by their growing closeness. The marriage wasn't over, after all—on the contrary, it was better than ever.

She was in the rose garden of their home in Virginia one afternoon, snipping what would be the last roses of the year. It was the end of November, and there was a damp chill in the air. She had just cut a partly opened bud from the Peace rosebush when Trock walked up to her carrying a package. Cady stopped what she was doing to watch the two dogs who had been following her turn to greet the attendant with soft barks and wagging tails.

"You've even won Hobo to your side, Trock." Cady smiled at him and took the proffered package, not looking at it. "Did you ever think these two would become friends?" She looked down at the bull terrier sitting side by side with the Doberman, their tongues hanging out of their mouths as though they were grinning at her and understood what she was saying.

The two animals were quite a contrast. The bull terrier was snow white now, almost all the scars healing nicely though the gash on his nose still had a redness to it, and his slanted eyes had a contented intelligence. Cady's research on the breed had revealed that despite their ability to fight ferociously, they were gentle animals, good as pets for both adults and children.

At first the two male canines had given each other a wide berth. There had been a hostile wariness in their manner, especially on the part of the Doberman, who resented the intruder to his home. Gradually his reluctant acceptance gave way to a cautious camaraderie that grew every day.

Trock watched the two dogs in silence for a time. Then he inclined his head and patted each animal, his facial muscles moving in the semblance of a smile. "Maybe not at first. Graf was determined not to let anyone disturb his domain, but when he found Hobo equally determined, they both backed down. Dogs are smarter than people." Trock took a deep breath, making Cady smile. He was not a man who liked speeches, and he would open up with no one except Cady or Rafe. He pointed to the parcel in her hand. "They said it was special delivery." Then he frowned at Cady. "You've been out here long enough in the cold. I'll walk the dogs a bit. You take the flowers and go inside."

Cady looked down at the brown-paper-wrapped article in her hand. She turned it over to see if there was a return address. There wasn't. She shrugged, lifted the small pile of flowers into her basket, pocketed the rose snips in her coverall, and strolled to the library door. She set the package on Rafe's desk and carried the flowers to the kitchen, where the housekeeper took them from her and said she would wash them and bring them in a vase to the library if Mrs. Densmore would like to arrange them there.

Cady took her time showering and shampooing her hair. Her thoughts were on Rafe and the quiet dinner they would have together this evening. Bouillabaisse was one of his favorites, and Cady decided that they would also have New York State champagne and the French rolls that Rafe was addicted to.

She dressed with care. Rafe's tastes were uppermost in her mind as she donned a silky wool dress in a light purple that was one shade darker than her eyes. Her medium-heel slings were a brown kid and even more comfortable than sneakers. All at once she remembered the flowers that the housekeeper had put in the library to be arranged, and she hurried from the room and down the stairs.

The roses were there, next to the package. Checking first to see if the flowers had plenty of water, Cady decided she would open the parcel before doing the arranging.

The strapping tape was troublesome to remove, but she was finally able to unwrap the box. While she crumpled the paper and tape in her hands before throwing it in the waste basket, she looked curiously at the plain, unmarked box that appeared as though it might contain typing paper. Whatever could it be? She lifted the cover and froze. She could actually feel the blood in her body drain to her toes. Her hands and feet turned to ice. She stared at the nude picture of herself, her head thrown back, her hands touching her own body in a provocative way. She lifted the picture between thumb and forefinger to look closer and found another one underneath it. Sure that she must be hallucinating, she closed her eyes, then opened them again and resumed perusing the pile of photographs. Each was more shocking than the last.

There were more horrors under the first five pictures of Cady alone in promiscuous poses. These were followed by pictures of Cady and . . . Oh, God! Cady felt the contents of her stomach rise. She ran for the tiny powder room off the library and threw up her lunch.

With shaking hands she wiped her face and looked at the chalk-faced person who stared back at her in the mirror. The purple bruises that were her eyes held a wounded look. How could it be? How could there be pictures of her and Rob Ardmore in lascivious poses? She staggered back to Rafe's desk in the library, not even glancing at the hapless roses. There were more pictures of her and Rob and . . . Cady almost fainted. There were pictures of her and Todd Leacock! What was going on? With lifeless fingers she picked up the typewritten sheet that had fluttered to the floor when she had picked up one of the pictures.

MRS. DENSMORE: YOU SHOULD BE ASHAMED OF YOURSELF. THESE PICTURES WILL BE SENT TO DAY MAGAZINE. PEOPLE NEED TO KNOW HOW CORRUPT YOU PEO-PLE CAN BE. YOU'LL RECEIVE A PHONE CALL THIS EVENING AT SEVEN P.M.

Cady stared at the typed words, not really comprehending. When the phone rang at her elbow, she let out a little scream.

"Cady, love, it's me. I have to see Conroy on the Elkins land scheme. It looks like it will run late. Forgive me? Cady?"

"Yes . . . of course, Rafe. I understand."

"Angel, is something wrong?"

"No . . . Good-bye."

Cady could sense Rafe's hesitancy, so she hung up quickly. Putting her face in her hands, she began to shake. Who could have done this? Why?

She managed to put Mrs. Lacey off when the house-keeper wanted to serve her some food. When Trock asked to see her, Cady told Mrs. Lacey to tell him she was busy. She sat in the darkening library, the box with the pictures clutched close to her stomach.

When the housekeeper rang at seven to tell her there was a call, Cady lifted the phone as though it had suddenly turned into a rattlesnake. "Yes, this is Cady Densmore."

"Recognize my voice, Cady? It's Todd Leacock."

Cady snapped straight in her chair, thinking of the pictures she held in her hand, remembering the photos of her and Todd. "Why are you calling here?" She couldn't seem to clear the hoarseness from her throat as she waited with a sense of doom for his answer.

"Come on, Cady. You were always such a smart girl in college. Prudish, but smart." Todd's laugh was harsh.

"Did you send those pictures?" Cady fought the quaver in her voice.

"Admit you never looked lovelier, Cady."

She could almost see the leer on his face. "I never posed for those pictures. You could go to prison for doing such a thing."

"I remember you posing for them, Cady. I remember photographing you and Congressman Ardmore, too. You never seemed to mind being seen naked with him."

"You're a liar." Cady tried to stifle the spasm in her mouth by biting her lips.

"It's your word against mine, lady. I have nothing to lose if these pictures come out. You do."

"What are you saying?" Her lips were pasteboard.

"I'm saying that I don't mind if the pictures become public knowledge. If you do, then you should be willing to cooperate with the electorate in your state. There are certain things we want done, and your husband is dragging his heels. If you persuade him to help us in our endeavors . . . then you can have the pictures and the negatives and do what you want with them."

"There are laws to punish blackmailers in this country." Cady licked her lips. They felt like papier-mâché.

"Don't use dirty words, Cady," Todd warned. "I get angry when people try to push me around."

"You're crazy," she whispered. "You know those pictures are faked. Why are you doing this?"

"I told you. A few people and myself want your husband to back down on this environmental bill for the Hudson and Lake Ontario. That's all we want, Cady. You can handle that. After all, it means more work for the state, more money——"

"To line the pockets of certain men with vested interests, such as Greeley and his boys," Cady hissed, her voice grim.

"I didn't mention any names, Cady."

"You didn't have to. This is a crime, Todd. Get out of it while you——"

"You talk to me about crime! You and all that Densmore money! Why should you have so much and I have so little? Do you think old Emmett Densmore made his money honestly? Damn it, you know he didn't. So what's the difference if I dip into the honey pot for my share?"

"You know it's wrong. Todd, listen to——"

"No, you listen, Cady. Get your husband to back down or the pictures come out. I'm not kidding."

The phone slammed in Cady's ear, making her blink. She held the receiver in her hand until she heard the dial tone, then she set it very carefully on the cradle. Wrapping her arms around her body, she sat there rocking, pulling herself into a nearly fetal position. Her mind fragmented into panic, frozen into stillness. Perhaps if Rafe had come home at that moment, she would have blurted out the whole thing to him, poured her anguish and fears into the open, but she was alone.

She had no concept of time passing when her hand reached for the telephone. She dialed the number in a stupor, almost surprised when she heard Rob Ardmore's voice. She had to tell him he was involved in this. He said hello twice before she responded. "It's Cady, Rob. I'm in terrible trouble." Her mouth had difficulty with the words, but finally she was able to tell Rob the bare outline of what had happened.

"Cady. Cady, listen to me. Don't give in. I'm coming

over right away. There's always a way to fight this sort of thing."

For the second time that evening the phone went dead in her ear before her numb arm had replaced the receiver.

She paced the library, head down, while she waited for Rob, her mind like cotton wool, barely functioning as she dealt with horrible visions of the future.

When she heard Rob's car in the drive, she answered the door herself. Mutely she stared at him, unable to control the shaking of her limbs.

Rob stepped forward, taking her by the arm and turning her back toward the library, only speaking after he had closed the door. "Cady, don't look like that." He put his arms around her. "We'll fight them."

"How?" she croaked, her hands clutching at his shirt front. "You haven't seen the pictures. They're awful. I'm ashamed to show them to you."

He set her away from him and looked around the room, seeing the box on the desk. In two strides he had the pictures in his hands, peering at them in scowling silence. "Whoever did these was no amateur." Rob ground the words out, looking up at her with a pronounced pallor on his face. "You must see that we can't submit to any of their demands. It would be a never-ending cycle of destruction. Next it would be some other bill that Rafe was interested in, or something I backed. There would be no end to it. You see that, don't you, Cady?"

She nodded in numb affirmation. "What can we do, then?"

Rob looked at her for a moment, shaking his head. "I need time to think." He exhaled deeply. "First we need someone we can trust who will watch this Leacock person. We have to find out whom Leacock is acting for." Rob looked at her for long moments. "I can think of a few people who would profit if I went down the tube. Who would stand to do well if Rafe was discredited?"

"Greeley," Cady pronounced, straightening. "And I

know someone I can trust." She strode to the door, feeling the blood rise in her face, and pressed the buzzer.

Trock arrived in short order, and though Cady didn't show him the pictures, she told him about Todd's phone call and what Rob had suggested they do.

Trock never took his gaze from her. His face was like a rock, but his eyes took on a strange fire as he listened to her. "I'll trail him, Mrs. D. I'll know when he breathes. Don't worry." He turned away, then paused at the door and turned back. "Is the senator not to know?"

Cady shrugged and shook her head. "I don't know."

"Let's see what the three of us can do with this first," Rob advised.

Trock nodded once and left the room.

Cady promised Rob she would find any excuse to put Todd off until they could find a way of undermining him. A few minutes later Rob left. When she had closed the door after him, Cady leaned against the sturdy oak, feeling her head pound. She sighed and straightened before going upstairs.

When the door leading to the back hall crashed open, she stared open-mouthed. Rafe was standing there like a boxer ready to come out of his corner.

"Damn it, Cady, what the hell is going on?" His hands opened and closed, his eyes glittering. "I saw Ardmore's car come out our gate just as I was coming up the road. What the hell do you mean carrying on like that?"

All the terror, the pain, the boiling confusion of the past hours erupted from her mouth. "Don't you speak to me like that! How dare you come on like the oh-so-moral husband with me? You of all people have no right to criticize anything I do," she lashed at him, anger throbbing in her ears.

"I'm your husband," Rafe roared, his body taking on a menacing curve.

"And you only remember that when it's convenient to you! How dare you not trust me!" Cady screamed at him, the frustrations of the evening pouring over her like hot lava, scorching her good sense. "I don't have to take that from a philanderer like you, a man who was the star attraction at those parties at Durra, going from woman to woman," she blurted, knowing she was being unfair.

Rafe bared his teeth, seeming to swell in size. His voice was like forged steel plunged into ice. "Philanderer? That's an archaic word for you, isn't it, lady? Why don't you say what you mean? You want trust, but you damn well never give it." He bit off the words and spat them at her like rivets from a gun.

"What would I trust about you? Should I trust that the first chance you get you would have another get-together with all your party friends at Durra?" She lifted her fists and shook them at him.

"You never gave me a chance to explain about Durra." Rafe's words sliced the air.

"You had every chance in the world to tell me about Durra, before and after we were married." Her trembling yell seemed to echo through the crystal of the chandelier and dig itself into the very plaster of the walls.

"I explained that to you."

"No, you excused yourself."

"Now you had better tell me what Rob Ardmore is doing in my home when I'm not here." He stepped toward her.

"I'll tell you nothing." Cady ran to the stairway. Half-way up, she turned to look down at him. "Nothing, do you hear me? And don't you ever come near me again. Never." She stumbled on the last stair but kept on running until she had slammed the bedroom door behind her.

She didn't bother to turn on the light as she stripped the clothes from her body and strewed them every which way. She threw herself naked on the bed, the raw burning of her eyes increasing as the tears bottled up behind them.

She lay there in the vortex of the nightmare, eyes wide open, wounds fissuring inside her, with nothing to comfort and soothe the pain.

Sleep came with the pink-streaked dawn, but the nightmare stayed with her.

*   *   *

The next day she was up at seven, after having slept for only two hours. She heard Rafe moving about in their suite, but she didn't leave her own room until she was sure he was gone. A long, cold shower didn't take the puffiness from her face, but the needle-sharp spray helped to bring her mind out of hiding.

She was on her second pot of coffee, having ignored the toast and eggs Mrs. Lacey set before her, when Trock walked into the dining room, the dogs at either side of him.

"I'll be gone most of the day. I'm taking Graf with me."

"What are you going to do?" Cady forced the words past numbed lips.

"No plan yet." Trock turned back to the door after telling Hobo to stay. His back to her, he added, "Don't worry."

"Thank you, Trock." Cady felt better. She called Hobo to her and walked outside to think. She went over and over in her mind what Todd had said to her. How had Greeley connected up with Todd Leacock? She closed her eyes, picturing their conversation on the day of the clambake. What had he said? That he'd done some work for people who worked for Rafe, she recalled as she walked down to the paddock, Hobo at her heels.

She stopped so abruptly that the dog at her side whined up at her. Bruno! Would he dare do this? Wouldn't Emmett balk at anything that might damage his son's political career? Cady nodded. The answer was an unqualified affirmative. She started walking again, feeling her mouth compress. Emmett wouldn't cross the street to save her life, but as long as she was Rafe's spouse, he wouldn't do anything that would spot her reputation. Emmett would jump off a skyscraper to see that his son remained a senator. Therefore, Cady thought in bitter amusement, Emmett would not have had a hand in the blackmail scheme. But would Bruno go it alone on something like this? Cady nodded again. He had the nerves of a riverboat gambler. "Bruno." She hissed the name, startling the bull terrier into whining and rubbing his muzzle against her thigh. Cady patted the animal absentmindedly. Would Bruno have the gall to cross Emmett in such a way? Yes. There were enormous sums of money involved if Greeley succeeded in burying the environmental bill before it reached the floor of the Senate.

"How do I prove such a thing, Hobo?" she quizzed the whining dog. "How do I throw a wrench in the works of a plan that would be disastrous to Rafe...to me...and to our marriage? If they're allowed to get away with this, Hobo, they'll begin to undermine all the hard-fought battles Rafe has engaged in for our state." She stopped, clenching her hands in front of her, seeing in her mind's eye Rafe brought down, disgraced by these men. "No!" she shouted, making the dog bark. She patted his head. "I'm not going to let it happen, Hobo. They would pull Rafe apart, just as you were torn apart in pit fighting. Right now I'm between a rock and a hard place"—Cady hit the palm of her hand with her fist—"but I will be damned if I'll let these people destroy Rafe or his ideals."

She paced back and forth in the meadow surrounding the paddock, racking her brain. "Stacy. Stacy Lande. I'll talk to her." Cady inhaled, feeling suddenly lighter as she thought of the secretary in Rafe's office whom she had hired away from Bruno Trabold at Stacy's own pleading. At first Cady had been very suspicious of the woman, thinking that she was a plant Bruno had placed there so he could spy on Cady. Gradually she had come to accept Stacy and believe her story that she could no longer work for the unscrupulous Bruno Trabold and still sleep nights. The two women had become close, and Cady considered her a good friend.

She returned to the house on the run and called Rafe's office, asking to speak to the secretary. "Stacy? It's Cady Densmore. Yes, it's been awhile." Cady took a deep breath. "Stacy, I want you to do a favor for me. I want..." Cady swallowed. "I want you to tell me more about the Durra parties. Yes, I know I said it was a dead issue...Now I need to know some things. I'd rather not talk about it on the phone. Yes, I know it was a rough time for you . . . for me, too." Cady gulped. "Stacy, I have it on good authority that there is a plot to destroy the senator and his work. You'll help me? Thank you. Yes, Robert's will be fine. One o'clock on Monday."

The rest of the morning Cady made notes on people she might have alienated while she was working in Rafe's office. The list wasn't long, but it held more names than she would have guessed had someone asked her beforehand.

When Trock returned, a panting Graf at his side, he held a camera out to her. "I brought this a while back. For a time I was an air photographer in the Marine Corps. Learned a few things." He paused, his throat working. "Leacock seems to know many people." He looked down at the dog. "Graf spotted his enemy . . . Bruno Trabold. They met on the access road to the Battle of Manassas Field. It's pretty open there, so I wasn't able to get too close . . ." He patted the dog. "But this fellow recognized Trabold and so did I." He coughed. "Following Todd Leacock hasn't been too hard. Don't imagine he figured anyone would do that. Got some good pictures of him and Trabold." He wrinkled his brow, clearing his throat as though talking made it hurt. "I won't be around here much. I want to see what Leacock does with his evenings." He took a deep breath. "Can you stall him?"

Cady nodded, grim-faced. "I will. I must."

Trock grunted. "Don't expect to see me until I have more information. The pictures will be ready tomorrow. I'm developing them myself."

"Thank you, Trock."

"They won't get away with it, Mrs. D." Trock's voice was flat, but there was a lethal flicker in his opaque eyes.

Rafe called and left a message with Mrs. Lacey that he would be working late that evening. Cady was both relieved that she could put off facing him after the row they'd had the previous evening and fearful that Rafe would be with a beautiful woman who would take his mind off his hysterical wife. All the pain of rejection that she had felt prior to Rafe's accident seemed to gather and balloon inside her once more. Worms of doubt nibbled away at the newfound happiness that she was beginning to find with her husband.

She plunged herself, dry-eyed, into the work at hand. She wouldn't allow herself ever again to become so immobilized by pain that she would retreat into a cocoon of oblivion. No! she lectured herself. Cady Nesbitt Densmore, you're a fighter, not a quitter! You can't give in to this! If you had talked to Rafe all those times before the accident, if you had told him how hurt you were by the things his family said and did to you, if you had made him talk to you instead of sending him alone to parties, to socials, then you might never have felt frozen out of his life. She gritted her teeth, nodding her head jerkily. Bruno Trabold and Todd Leacock expect you to cave in. Surrender! Concede! Cady surged to her feet behind the desk, rocking the heavy oak desk chair. "Rafe didn't quit," she muttered, staring at the oak-paneled walls, her hands snapping the pencil they held between them. "I won't quit, either. I'll see them in hell first!"

She was staring sightlessly down at the pieces of pencil in her hand when the phone rang. "Yes?"

Todd Leacock spoke in her ear. "Have you got what we want, Cady?"

"I need more time." She tried to moisten her dry lips with her tongue. "Rafe will be suspicious if I tackle him with this all at once. I have to move slowly or he'll know that something is wrong. I can't hurry Rafe into changing his mind on the bill." She held her breath.

"All right, Cady." Todd's voice had a surly tinge. "But you don't have too much time. My friend tells me that some congressmen have already caucused on the environmental bill. Time to get moving, Cady."

And who else but Bruno would tell you that, you rat, Cady thought, feeling her face twist with anger. She took a deep breath. "All right, I'll work on him."

When she replaced the receiver, her hand shook. She hadn't realized it was possible for her to feel as much venom against another person.

Bruno was jealous of Rafe! It was as though a light had gone on in her head. He hated Rafe because of the money and prestige that were Rafe's and could never be his! She could recall with great clarity the way Bruno had always looked at her husband—that hooded cobra look. Bruno's great chance had been when Rafe had had the accident. She felt sure now that Bruno would at some time have tried to run for Rafe's seat, with Emmett's backing. Bruno hated Rafe now, because he was well and Bruno couldn't take over his Senate seat. Cady pressed her hands to her mouth, feeling sick.

When the phone rang again, she jumped, staring at the instrument as though it had turned into a tarantula. "Yes?"

"Cady? It's Rob." His voice seemed to have an excited lift to it. "Cady, I think I hit pay dirt. It seems Greeley has been getting pretty desperate. He has a great deal of his own and his friends' money riding on the defeat of the environmental bill. He's really turning on the pressure on the Hill and has tried to put the screws on Emmett Densmore. Emmett balked at that, but it seems that Bruno Trabold is hand in glove with Greeley on this."

Cady nodded as she listened, then proceeded to tell Rob what Trock had told her about the meeting of the two men at the Battle of Manassas marker and the pictures he took. She also told him about her conversation with Todd.

"Cady, I think we're going to get them on this." Rob sounded almost gleeful. Then his voice changed. "If Rafe should find out, if somehow your marriage is jeopardized by all this, remember you always have me. I love you, Cady. And I think you could care for me."

"Of course I care for you, Rob..." Cady looked up as the library door swung open. Her husband stood there, his eyes steel-blue and murderous. "Rob, I have to go."

"Is it Rafe? Is he there? Cady, will you be all right?"

"Yes, yes, I'll be fine. Good-bye." Cady replaced the receiver, not taking her eyes from her husband. "It's not what you think."

"And what do I think?" The quiet menace in Rafe's voice filled the room. "I said once that I would never keep you if you decided that you wanted to go." The words fired from his mouth like bullets. "I've changed my mind. You're my wife and I'll see you and your lover—"

Cady slapped the leather desk mat in front of her with both hands and jumped to her feet. "I don't have a lover!"

"—in hell first. Now you damn well stay away from Rob Ardmore or I'll go to his office and take him apart in front of the whole House of Representatives."

"You . . . you hooligan! How dare you threaten a congressman! Who the hell do you think you are, anyway?"

"I'm your husband!" Rafe shouted, anger propelling him further into the room as he threw down his coat and slammed the door in one angry motion.

"All of a sudden you remember that!" Cady shouted back, wondering why they were doing this again. "What about all those times you left me alone to go to those damn parties? What were you then? A loving husband?"

"You sent me to parties alone. You refused to accompany me. What did you want me to do?" he grated.

"I sure didn't want you acting like the sultan of Washington, going from bed to bed to bed." Cady's voice cracked she was so angry.

"Cady." Rafe seemed to swell. "How dare you say such a thing to me? I was never unfaithful to you."

"Liar!" Cady roared. Then she could have bitten off her tongue, longing to call back that hated word.

"I never lied to you." Rafe's face was the color of putty, his lips rock hard as they formed around the words. He spun on his heel and left the room.

"Rafe . . . oh Rafe, don't go," Cady whispered as she heard him take the stairs two at a time.

* * *

Cady had another sleepless night. Twice she rose and went to the door between their rooms, wanting to tell him what happened. Twice she reached the door, leaned against it for a few moments, then retraced her steps to bed.

The next morning she felt as if she'd just placed last in a marathon. She stumbled out of bed and into the shower. Only when she was gasping and beginning to turn blue did she step out and dry herself. She sighed as she dressed in lavender corduroy jeans and vest and went down for coffee. Hopefully she would hear more from Trock today. She had the uneasy feeling that she couldn't put Todd off for too long.

She stopped open-mouthed when she walked into the morning room and saw Rafe still at the table, the paper in front of him, a coffee cup in his hand. He leaned over and filled her cup from the silver pot, then rose to hold out her chair, his face impassive.

"Sit down, Cady."

"I thought you would be gone."

"No doubt." Rafe shook his paper, then lifted the coffee cup to his mouth. "We're invited to Durra for dinner tonight. I accepted for both of us." He held up his hand as she glowered at him. "Before you tear into me, let me explain that it's just the family. It's not a political gathering of any kind. My father pointed out that we haven't been to Durra since my recovery. He feels it's about time we all had dinner as a family."

"I see." She took a sip of the scalding brew, burning her tongue. She reached for the water glass, trying to soothe the pain. "And will Bruno be there?"

Rafe frowned at her. "I don't know. Maybe." He shrugged. "You shouldn't let Bruno bother you. He has nothing to do with us anymore. Ignore him."

"Bruno is rather hard to ignore," Cady muttered, wishing she could tell Rafe just exactly how hard it was. She had a horror of her husband ever seeing the box of pictures locked away in her file cabinet.

Rafe pushed his plate aside, making Cady's brow crease as she noticed how little he had eaten. When he lit one of his cheroots, the crease in her forehead deepened.

"Trock doesn't like you smoking those."

"Trock—I haven't seen the man in a couple of days. Where has he been? I looked for him in the gym last night and again this morning."

Cady stared at her husband, feeling her neck redden. "I suppose he must have a life of his own."

Rafe gazed at her through the curl of smoke. "I suppose. I haven't seen Graf, either. Did Trock take him along?" He looked down at the sleeping Hobo lying at his feet and missed the start that Cady gave at his words.

"Ah . . . he could have. The dog likes to ride in the car."

"Yes, I suppose." He pressed the cheroot, not even half-smoked, into the ashtray and rose to his feet. "So I'll assume that we'll be going to Durra?"

"Ah . . . yes."

"Well, then . . . have a good day." Rafe stopped next to her chair.

Cady looked out the window, afraid if she met Rafe's eyes she would dissolve into tears, sink to her knees, grab hold of his legs and beg him not to throw her away when he saw the horrible pictures of her. "You have a nice day, too."

She heard him smother an oath as he left, and she began to tremble.

8

CADY DRESSED THAT evening like a somnambulist. Even the cold shower she had stood under for fifteen minutes didn't lift her spirits.

Todd had called her that afternoon. His demands had increased. Now they wanted Rafe to throw his weight behind more defense spending. It hadn't taken Cady long to see through that ploy, since she knew Emmett and Bruno and their friend Greeley had oil interests in the Middle East and Africa. Speculation drilling on the Dark Continent was expensive, not just the equipment but also the mercenary army they felt they must maintain to protect themselves against insurgents who attacked them at every turn. If they involved the United States government in their quarrels, it would certainly lessen the personal expense. She wanted to scream at Leacock that she knew whom he was working for and what they were after. Somehow she had managed to keep cool and not show her fury at his attempted manipulations. Somehow she

133

had managed to fob him off again with excuses that Rafe had to be handled with kid gloves or he would discover what they were doing and have no compunction about bringing the whole sordid mess into the open.

Rafe was late coming home that night, but that wasn't unusual these days. It seemed he spent a great deal of time avoiding her.

Cady looked in the mirror, surprised to see that she was dressed and had all her makeup on. She studied the deep gold silk dress whose antique finish was only one hue deeper than her hair. With it she decided to wear the amethyst necklace and earring set that Rafe had bought for her when they had returned from their honeymoon twelve long years ago. The settings for the pale purple drop earrings were an antique gold almost the shade of her dress, a sheath with no adornment except its dramatic, almost off-the-shoulder neckline. Her heels were a light tan kid with medium heels and sling backs. She had a change purse in matching kid hanging from a chain. This she slung over her shoulder.

She stiffened when she heard Rafe moving around in his room. It wasn't until she could hear the shower that she left her own room and descended to the library. She knew it was childish, but the less she saw Rafe, the less guilt she felt about the pictures and the underhanded methods she, Rob, and Trock were employing to set things right.

She walked to the hidden bar in the bookcase, pressed the switch, waited for the doors to swing open and the light to come on, then poured herself some Riesling over ice cubes. She was sipping the sharp wine when the phone rang. The buzzer sounded twice, signaling that it was for her. She picked up the desk phone.

"Cady? I hope this isn't a bad time to call, but I've discovered something that might help us."

"Just a moment, Rob." Cady set the phone down and closed the door. "There. I won't be able to talk long. Rafe will be down in a minute. What is it?"

"The man I have digging into things has come up with

a little item that will interest the voters of New York. It seems our friend Bruno Trabold is equal partners with one Silas Greeley—our lobbyist Greeley—on a land deal on the Hudson River. They stand to make a great deal of money if a proposed nuclear power plant is built on said site."

"The rat! The double-dyed rat," Cady muttered into the phone. "That Judas." She took a deep breath. "I wonder if my father-in-law knows that his fair-haired boy is feathering his own nest."

"My informant sees no evidence that Emmett is involved in this, and I asked him specifically if there was a connection." Rob seemed to be reading from something. "Cady, if you can just hold them off for a few more days, I think we may be able to nail the whole nasty bunch. If we're lucky, we'll be able to do it without those damn pictures ever having to surface."

"I hope so, Rob. Thank you so much for everything. I don't know what I would have done without you."

Cady replaced the phone as her husband pushed the door open wide.

His face was a gray mask of fury. A muscle jumped under his left eye; his hands clenched and unclenched. "You tell Ardmore for me that if he calls here again, I'll break his damn neck. And *you* stay away from *him*." His voice was like sandpaper rubbed on slate.

Cady lifted her chin, hoping her face gave no hint that her insides had turned to jelly. "Rob is a friend of mine—a good friend. If you don't like my friends calling me here at your home—"

"This is your home, too," Rafe thundered, his teeth bared.

"—then I'll move to where my friends can feel free to call me." Cady felt as though her skin were quivering loose from her flesh.

"Don't you ever speak like that again!" Rafe ground the words at her. "You're not leaving me."

Relief at his words almost caved her in, but she lifted her chin still higher, not wanting him to know how tearfully grateful she was that he didn't want her to leave. "Then don't you dare dictate to me who should call me here. I don't tell you whom you should speak to. Don't tell *me*."

"And would you like it if I had women calling here?" Rafe shot back at her.

"What do you mean, if? They have called," she fired in return.

"That's a damn lie! No woman ever called me here after we married."

"That's the lie," Cady snapped, fighting against the wobble in her voice. "Lee Terris called here more than once asking for you." Her lips pressed together as she regretted the words. The last thing she wanted was for Rafe to discover the hurt that lay like a heavy weight deep inside her.

Rafe stared at her, shaking his head. "Why would Lee call here? We have nothing to talk about. The only times I've seen Lee have been when I went to Durra to see my father."

"Ah, yes, good old Durra, party house par excellence. Naturally you would see her there."

"Damn it, Cady, I meant I saw her there when I visited my father's home, not when I partied."

"For God's sake, don't try to explain Durra to me. I haven't got a devious enough mind to understand that setup." She gulped down the rest of her wine, glad that the ice had diluted it. She watched Rafe stare at the glass, then back at her face.

"You rarely drink anything," he said.

"You and your family will probably drive me to alcoholism," she snapped. "Shall we go? I doubt there's sufficient wine in all of California and New York together to dull my nerves enough to stand an evening with your family." She sailed past him to the front door.

"I might find agreement with you there," Rafe pronounced dryly, holding the door for her, then taking her arm to lead her to the car.

At any other time the drive through the edge of Maryland hunt country with its stone fences and rolling green hills would have entranced Cady, but as usual just the thought of going to Durra was enough to start her stomach rumbling and her attention centering on the ordeal of a dinner with the Densmores.

"Cady, would you like to stop somewhere and get something to eat just to stop your stomach from growling?" The amusement in Rafe's voice annoyed her.

"Sorry." She pressed her hand on her abdomen. "No, I don't want to stop." It rumbled again.

Rafe reached over and pressed his hand flat on her stomach, pushing her own out of the way. His fingers kneaded the slightly curved area above her lap.

She felt stiff at first, wanting to push away his hand, but she had neither the inclination nor the strength to do so. Soon the growling stopped, replaced by the noiseless rumble of sensations deep within her. She bit her lips to keep from pleading with Rafe to stop the car and make love to her right there beside the highway.

Rafe kept his hand on her the rest of the way, the heat from it penetrating right to her backbone. He lifted his hand only after they had left the highway and turned onto the meandering lane that would take them through the gates of Durra, up the crushed-rock drive to the colonnaded house that stood on a knoll overlooking beautiful fields. Today there were only a few horses to be seen, but Cady leaned forward to get a better look.

"Would you like to ride after dinner, Cady?"

"How long are we staying?" she asked warily.

Rafe shrugged. "Who knows? If it gets boring, we'll leave right after we eat."

Cady turned to look at him. "You'd do that?"

"I would." Rafe let the car come to halt on the circular drive, then turned to her. "I won't let my family bully you ever again, Cady. I think I told you that."

"Yes, you did. Thank you for that, Rafe." Cady turned away, fumbling at the latch on the door, not wanting him to see the tears that were gathering in her eyes.

"Cady? Cady, wait." He put his hand on her shoulder,

but she wouldn't turn to look at him. "Cady, can't we try again? We had something good..."

"Your family will be waiting, Rafe." Cady wrenched free, hearing his muttered oath behind her as she almost leaped from the car. She couldn't tell him that she wanted to be his sole love, that she not only wanted to try again, she wanted to try forever. But what if he saw the pictures? What would he say? How could she bear the contempt in his eyes. Suspicious of Rob Ardmore as Rafe was, how could she hope he would believe that the pictures were merely cleverly faked?

She skidded to a halt in front of the door just as Samson opened it. Samson was a fixture at Durra. He had been a prizefighter in his younger days. His real name was Kieron O'Malley, and he had come from the same section of Ireland as Emmett's people, County Cork. He had retired from the fight ring many years ago, but his professional name, Samson, had stuck, and that was how all visitors to Durra referred to him. He was one of the few people at her father-in-law's home whom Cady felt comfortable with.

"Lady Cat'leen, how are you? Come in. If it ain't his lordship roight behind you. Rafe, boyo, how are you?" Samson laughed as he crushed Rafe's hand in his and the two of them stood there squeezing for all they were worth. It was a foregone conclusion that Samson's ham-like hands would win, but, Cady noted with satisfaction, Rafe held his own, making Samson's color rise. "*Spalpeen!*" He used the Gaelic slang invective with a grin. "You're stronger, that's for sure." He turned to look at Cady.

Before Samson could ask his usual question, she spoke. "No, there's nothing in the oven yet." And she poked her tongue at the bluff Irishman when both he and Rafe burst out laughing.

"And are you so sure, colleen? You have a different look to you, I'd swear to it." Samson laughed harder at the flush on her face.

Rafe didn't laugh. He stared at Cady as though he

would see deep inside her. He had opened his mouth to speak when a yell from the stairs turned all heads that way.

"Hey, you two, it's about time you arrived. I'm starved." Gareth clattered down the stairs and flung himself at his older brother, trying to wrestle him to the floor. Before he had gotten Rafe into a grip, Cady was there cuffing him behind the ear. "Ouch, Cady. What the hell is the matter with you?"

"It's one thing for Samson to hand wrestle Rafe, but *you* are not going to knock him to the ground." She shook her finger in her brother-in-law's face. "He isn't that strong yet, and I'm not going to stand by and let you undo all the good work that has been done on Rafe just because you're an overgrown puppy." She put her hands on her hips and glowered up at Gareth, who rubbed the back of his ear sheepishly.

Gareth glanced at Rafe and shrugged. "You married a tiger, brother; you'd better watch out. If she decides to come after you, she'll chew you up."

"The only way I'll go after Rafe is if he doesn't take care of his health," Cady said haughtily. Gareth put his nose in the air, trying to imitate her. When she moved to cuff him again, he ducked, and Rafe caught her around the waist.

"You'll have my baby brother covered with bruises, darling." Rafe bent over her, nibbling her ear.

"Cady's right." Gavin came down the stairs in a much more sedate fashion than his ebullient twin. "Rafe's health is the primary thing. If you weren't such a thug, Gareth, you'd know it, too." Gavin smiled as his twin came at him in a crouch, meeting him halfway. Though he was of slighter build than his twin, he was faster and more coordinated.

They wrestled in the front hall as their father descended the formal curved staircase that made a better setting for an antebellum Southern ball than a wrestling match.

"You two get up from there," Emmett said mildly,

watching with obvious pleasure as his progeny bounced off the walls with groans and thuds. "Rafe, my boy, how are you?"

"Fine, and my wife is fine as well." Rafe took his father's outstretched hand in his, his other arm pulling Cady close to his side.

"Oh? That's good." Emmett looked at Cady in the circle of Rafe's arm and a frown appeared between his eyes. "Lee Terris is here for dinner. I know you'll be glad to hear that, Rafe."

"It's your house. Ask whom you please." Rafe's voice had an edge of irritation that narrowed his father's gaze on him. But before he could say anything, the door leading to Emmett's study opened, revealing Bruno Trabold. Emmett turned to look at him, smiling. "And you'll stay, too, won't you, Bruno?"

"Since it's family, I won't stay." Bruno smiled at Emmett, his hooded gaze touching on the rest of the persons gathered there.

"You're the same as family," Emmett roared.

"Not to me, he isn't," the irrepressible Gareth stated, staring back at his glowering father.

"Me, either," Gavin echoed.

"Where are your manners?" Emmett glared at the twins, but he accompanied Bruno to the front door.

Neither Cady nor Rafe had spoken to Bruno, and he had not acknowledged them.

Lee Terris floated from the back of the house in time to say she was disappointed that Bruno wasn't staying. He was such a stimulating conversationalist. Then she shrugged and walked straight to Rafe.

Gareth stepped in front of her, catching her uplifted arms, then gripping her in a bear hug. "I love it when you get physical, Lee, baby." He gave her a resounding smack on the lips.

Although Lee smiled when Gavin laughed, Cady could see the angry glitter in her eyes.

Emmett herded them into the ballroom-size front room, where the priceless Sheraton furniture that had been collected by Rafe's mother was interspersed with overstuffed couches that would bear the weight of men like the Densmores, who demanded comfort over style.

Samson served the drinks. He was quick to make Cady's mineral water and lime and serve it to her even as Emmett muttered about the milksop swill drunk by his daughter-in-law. The boys drank beer. Lee Terris had a martini. Rafe and his father drank Irish whiskey with no ice and little water.

When Rafe's sisters arrived in a swirl of children and subdued husbands, Samson bustled about fixing drinks for them as well. He made a pitcher of sweet Manhattans for Aileen and Aveen and their husbands. For the children—two boys and a girl—he poured root beer that he himself had made into old-fashioned glass mugs.

"Cady, that dress! It's lovely." Aveen said it as if she were offended.

Gareth crept up behind Cady. "What a traitor you are, Cady. Being well dressed when you should look dowdy." His voice went an octave higher. "My dear, you will never get along in this world if you're going to be fashionable, intelligent, and gorgeous." His voice was loud enough so that both Aveen and Aileen looked at him and frowned.

"Don't be a bigger fool than you can help, Gareth," Aileen said repressively, looking at him down her long, thin nose.

"Don't try any of those schoolmarm airs with me, sister dear," Gareth shot back. "I'm not your husband . . . and I won't be trounced on by your size-ten shoes."

Aileen seemed to swell. Gareth's chin jutted forward. Gavin made a move toward his twin. Cady stared at Aileen's husband, David Bailey. His face had taken on an ugly crimson cast as he looked from his brother-in-law to his wife and back again.

Without thinking, Cady walked to Dave's side and took hold of his arm. He looked down at her, an angry glitter in his eyes. "I don't know how you've kept from tying her up and putting her in the attic all these years,"

Cady said lightly, grinning up at him.

He put one hand over hers, his expression relaxing. "Maybe that's exactly what I *will* do." He looked back at his wife, who now stood nose to nose facing her brother, their voices low but still piercing enough to have turned the heads of the children. "Aileen, shut up and sit down. Now." Dave's voice wasn't loud, but it penetrated the heated argument and the concentration of most of the others in the room. His two children, two-year-old Mara and ten-year-old Emmett, stared at their father, mouths agape, circles of root beer on their lips. Aileen started as though someone had stuck a pin in her. Emmett scowled. Aveen looked affronted; her husband, Harrison Colby, looked hopeful.

Aileen turned slowly away from a surprised Gareth, a wide-eyed Gavin at his side muttering, "That tears it." She drew herself up to her full height, her nostrils flaring as her mouth opened to speak.

"And don't bother to begin one of your long-winded discourses, either." Dave spoke through his teeth. "I'm fed up with it and I'm fed up with your damn argumentative family." He jabbed his finger at her. "And if you make one comment, I'll take the kids and get out of here and you can stay in this bear's den."

The silence would have been total if it weren't for Rafe going to the bar, pouring a drink, and carrying it to his brother-in-law, saluting him with it before handing it to him.

"What the hell do you mean talking to my daughter that way?" Emmett came alive out of his stunned silence.

"If you don't like it, I'll leave." Dave took a long swallow of his drink, the tremor in his hand barely discernible to Cady. "And if I do, I'm not coming back."

"How dare you!" Aveen sputtered, starting to step forward.

All at once Aveen's husband, Harrison, rose and took hold of her arm. "Mind your own business, Aveen. If you say anything else, I'll leave with Dave."

Rafe went back to the bar, made another drink, and

handed it to his other brother-in-law, saluting him in the same way.

Aileen and Aveen stared at their husbands while Emmett's color fluctuated from magenta to scarlet to putty.

Samson reentered the room, ran a quick eye around, cleared his throat, and announced, "Dinner. It's hot."

Dave took another swallow of his drink and offered his arm to Cady. Harrison came up on her other side and took hold of her other hand. "Warmonger," he whispered. "I haven't felt so good being at Durra in a long, long time." He grinned over her head at Dave. They strolled past Emmett through the double-doored archway into the spacious dining room. The others followed in desultory fashion.

When they were all seated, the children included, since Emmett insisted that his grandchildren dine with their elders when they came to Durra, Rafe rose to his feet, wineglass in hand. "I'd like to propose a toast. To my wife, Cady, who takes on all comers and wins." He gave Cady an enigmatic smile, then emptied his wineglass in two long swallows.

Her two brothers-in-law and the twins jumped to their feet as well and shouted, "To Cady," then quaffed their wine. Then they looked at the sisters and Emmett.

Emmett's mouth worked as though he had hot peppers in it, but he raised his glass and mumbled, "To Cady." Aileen and Aveen took deep breaths, watching their husbands as though they had turned into tigers before their eyes. "To Cady," the cold voices echoed. Lee Terris reluctantly did the same.

The conversation at dinner was not the usual. The norm at Durra was for Aileen and Aveen to hold forth on every subject, deferring only to their father. Tonight, as though someone had untied their tongues, Dave and Harrison took the conversational gambit between their teeth and worried it like puppies with a bone. Cady would have been deeply impressed with the knowledge and scope of her brothers-in-law if she hadn't been so immersed in her own misery.

After the first shock of hearing their in-laws discourse on the advantages of having technicians from Germany in their factories, Gavin and Gareth jumped in with their own animated accounts of skiing in Germany the previous year and how intrepid they had found the Germans on the slopes.

Cady laughed with the others from time to time, but she felt her husband's eyes on her, that blue-gray peeling back her skin and picking apart her mind. She was convinced that if Rafe chose to, he could indeed read her mind.

When dessert was offered, Cady declined, contenting herself with the grapes that accompanied the cheese board. Her stomach seemed to be doing flip-flops, and she had a full, uncomfortably swollen feeling.

All at once she sat straight up in her chair, heat rising from her toes and the tips of her fingers. She hadn't had a period in quite a while. Even discounting her totally irregular cycle, she should have had one by now. What was it Samson had said to her earlier? She had a different look to her tonight. Could that superstitious Irishman have seen what she hadn't yet guessed?

"My dear Cady, you look positively green," Lee Terris cooed from her place across the table. "I hope you're not going to condemn the cooking at Durra." The superbly groomed brunette sipped at her wine. "It doesn't seem to bother you if you insult the Densmores." The voice had a velvet lilt that just carried to Emmett's ears.

"I wouldn't like anyone coming to Durra and insulting me." He seemed still to be simmering from the actions of his sons-in-law.

Gavin leaned close to Cady, his body like a protective shield. "Cady didn't say anything." He looked over at Lee, his face contorting in dislike. "And I don't know where the hell you got the idea that *you* could come here and insult anyone. If you insult my sister-in-law, I'll take it personally."

Rafe's body seemed to stiffen as he caught fragments of what Gavin was saying. He was too far up the table to have heard it all, but the grim look on his face when he glanced from his brother to Lee boded ill for someone.

Lee looked at Rafe, her smile strained. "I think this silly conversation has gone far enough. Aileen, do tell us about the Christmas party planned at Bethesda."

"Don't forget the Christmas party I'm having here," Emmett interrupted. "Lee is helping me with it, and I expect you all to attend."

The evening wound down early. Cady had a feeling she wasn't the only one glad to see it come to an end.

On the drive home there was virtual silence between her and Rafe. When they reached the Highlands, she went directly to her room, not waiting for him to come into the house. She was glad to strip off her clothes and head for a warm bath. She took time to study her nude form in the three-way mirror in the bathroom. Her body didn't look any different, but somehow she knew it was. All at once she recalled the first night that she and Rafe had made love after his return from the hospital. That night she had thought she might be ovulating, but then she had forgotten about it. There had seemed so many other things to think about that she hadn't really considered it again.

She stepped into the frothy depths of the round tub that could easily accommodate four people and rested her head on the foam bath pillow. If only she didn't have Todd Leacock, Bruno, and those pictures to worry about, she could wallow in the joy of impending motherhood. For all at once she had no doubts. She was going to have Rafe's child. Oh, he would be happy enough about it. Rafe loved children, and their earlier failure to have any had been as big a disappointment to him as to Cady. But when he found out about those pictures, he would be monumentally angry. He would consider her unfit to raise a child, his child.

Cady sank up to her chin in suds, the sting of tears in her eyes. She would have nothing once Rafe found out. Nothing! She rose to a sitting position, causing a wave of water to wash up the sides of the tub. Damn it,

she wasn't going to go down without a fight. She would
take Bruno Trabold and Todd Leacock with her, even if
she never did another thing on this earth.

With that victory uppermost in her mind, she dragged
herself to bed to sink into a restless sleep. Rafe hadn't
said good night to her, she realized with a sigh just before
she closed her eyes.

Rafe was gone before she rose the next day and Cady
was glad, because a sudden attack of nausea sent her to
the bathroom in a rush. The sour taste left in her mouth
was not totally due to the nausea, but it kept her from
eating breakfast.

Trock came to tell her that he had found Greeley and
Leacock meeting at a restaurant. He had photographed
them, and he had also managed to place a recorder in
Leacock's car; though he hadn't yet retrieved the trans-
mitter, he felt it would hold enough to implicate Leacock
in wrongdoing. "You aren't eating." Trock's slate-gray
eyes reproached her as he rubbed the ears of the bull
terrier. Graf had placed his head in Cady's lap. She knew
the dog had missed her while he had been away with
Trock. "I told you not to worry," Trock accused her.

After he left, Cady toyed with a triangle of toast and
thought of her lunch with Stacy Lande.

At five minutes before one o'clock, Cady left her
Mercedes sports car in the parking lot of the posh French
restaurant called Robert's. There was a chance she'd be
seen by people she knew, perhaps even Bruno, but since
she and Stacy had always been friendly, she hoped that
anyone seeing them would think it was just an ordinary
women's luncheon. After all, Stacy was on Rafe's staff,
and Cady had been instrumental in getting her there.

Cady was fond of Stacy and had found her an efficient
secretary. Perhaps because she was the only person in
Rafe's office actually hired by Cady, the two women
had become close.

At the beginning of lunch they had much to say to
one another about people they had worked with. Cady

found the catching up amusing as Stacy recounted many anecdotes about the staff.

Stacy took a deep breath as she watched the waiter depart after pouring them more coffee. Then she looked at Cady. "I have a feeling you didn't ask me to meet you here to have me tell you about Senator Nielsen's Labrador running up and down the halls."

Cady smiled. "You're right." She pressed her napkin to her lips. "Stacy, I'm going to be very frank with you because I think I can trust you."

"You can."

"I'm being blackmailed." She exhaled, watching Stacy, who sat very still and returned her gaze. "I feel sure that Bruno is behind it. Do you think he's capable of it?"

Stacy took a deep breath, her thirty-five years resting lightly on her designer-suited shoulders. Her blond hair might have come from a bottle, but it was well done and had a soft richness. "Yes, I do. He not only *could* do it, Cady, he *has* done it to others. That's why I had to get away from there. We all have to compromise in some areas on the job, but working for Bruno was like working for the Syndicate." She took a sip of ice water and looked around the elegant restaurant. "To give the devil his due, I really don't think Emmett knew the extent of Bruno's shady dealings. Bruno Trabold is one of the most underhanded people I have ever known, and I wouldn't trust him around the corner."

"That's what I felt. And what about Silas Greeley?" Cady leaned both elbows on the table. "You once told me that Greeley pimped those parties at Durra." Cady bit her lip, fighting the sick feeling rising in her throat.

"Not just at Durra. Greeley and Bruno Trabold set up situations like that for many political galas. That's how they obtained a hold on so many legislators. I don't think Mr. Densmore ever knew that the women brought to the parties were prostitutes controlled by his closest business associate. Once I saw Bruno's little black book. In fact, I copied it on the sly to protect myself if he ever tried anything funny with me. Fortunately I never had to use it, but I brought the copies with me today, in case you need them." She smiled in response to Cady's slack-jawed look of surprise.

"I never expected anything like this, Stacy. Thank you."

"Listen, I saw how you were with Rafe when he was flat on his back. Rafe was good to me; he always treated me right." She frowned down at her napkin. "I saw how people tried to manipulate Rafe when he came to Durra...his father, who brought oil men to the house in order to pressure Rafe into not supporting a bill that would impose fines for oil spills, antienvironmental people, loggers, mining interests, and many others. Bruno harried Rafe constantly. They tried to turn Rafe into a puppet for their own uses, but they couldn't do it. Rafe is strong and he fought back. I remember how ashamed he was about the scandal at Durra and how he never tried to excuse himself. But from that day on there was no more hanky-panky with him. Long before he met you, Cady, Rafe had become the straight, honest legislator he is today."

Cady felt frozen to her seat. "You mean he didn't go to other orgies at Durra?"

Stacy shook her head vehemently. "There were no more orgies at Durra. Neither Emmett nor Rafe would have allowed it. Oh, Bruno's tried to get Rafe into compromising situations elsewhere, but Rafe would have none of it. If he went to a party that wasn't totally on the up and up, he left immediately, and he ignores his father's attempts to throw that scheming Lee Terris into his lap at every opportunity, too. This is what I tried to tell you when I came to work for you on Rafe's staff, but you didn't want to listen. I'm glad you're listening now. I owe you and Rafe a lot and I'd like to see the two of you happy."

"Thank you, Stacy." Cady smiled at the woman through a mist. She had believed what Bruno had said about Rafe, and she had called Rafe a liar, but Rafe hadn't been lying to her. "And, Stacy, thanks for the little book. If I can, I'm going to ruin Bruno Trabold." She gave the other woman a grim smile.

Stacy lifted her water glass. "To justice."

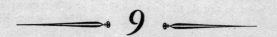

9

CADY CALLED DR. KELLMAN and asked him to recommend a good obstetrician. Her regular gynecologist no longer took obstetrical cases. When she met Dr. Green, she was a little taken aback by his youthful appearance, but within minutes they had established good rapport.

Cady went home overflowing with goodwill, her purse stuffed with vitamins, her mind's eye already picturing a dark-haired boy with deep blue eyes.

The phone was ringing as she passed the study. Her head was in the clouds when she answered.

"You sound pretty chipper today. Have you got what we want?" Todd's voice brought her back to earth with a crash.

"I told you Rafe won't be stampeded." Cady couldn't keep her voice from shaking.

"No more stalling, Cady. I'll call you back tonight and I'll want a firm answer about when your husband will begin blocking the environmental bill and cooperate on a few other matters." All at once there was harsh amusement in his voice. "Look in your mailbox, Cady. There's a package for you."

Cady didn't want to open the package, but she did. There were more pictures of her, making her gag. She opened the file drawer and pushed them in with the others.

That night at dinner Rafe seemed content to sit with her over coffee. Cady felt flustered by his presence. She needed time to think.

"I'll have my coffee in the library," she said, rising.

"All right. I'll join you." Rafe smiled, then reached for the silver tray.

"There's no need for you to bother," Cady said quickly. Her plan to speak to Trock was rapidly becoming impossible to execute. If he came to the library while Rafe was there, she would just have to put off the man.

"It's no bother." Rafe gestured to her to precede him as he easily held the heavy silver tray.

Cady settled down in one of the overstuffed leather chairs that stood at right angles to the fireplace, watching as Rafe set the tray on the small table between them.

They sat in silence while Cady poured, then handed a cup to Rafe. Still they didn't speak. Cady tried taking deep breaths to calm herself. She took a relieved breath when Rafe set down his cup and went to kneel in front of the fireplace, jabbing at a smoldering log with the poker to coax it to flame.

When the door to the library opened and Trock entered, Cady knew at once that he wasn't aware of Rafe's presence in the room, even though Graf bounded forward to nuzzle his master.

"Mrs. Densmore, I have the pictures with me and I was able to get the recorder from . . ." He paused, staring at Cady's frozen face.

When Rafe rose to his feet, frowning, Trock took a step backward as though he would retreat. "Trock, come here," Rafe rasped out. "What are you talking about?"

Trock swallowed but said nothing.

Cady stared at Rafe, seeing her whole life sweep down

the sewer that Bruno and Todd had created. "He won't answer you because I told him not to discuss this with you." She cleared her throat, her eyes heavy as she focused on her husband.

"Why did you tell him that?" Rafe's voice was gentle, but his eyes had a sapphire glitter.

"Because I'm being blackmailed." Cady coughed the words from her constricted throat.

Rafe let out a deep breath. "So that's it." He turned to Trock. "Come in and close the door." He put out his hand for the things Trock carried.

For a moment it looked as though the taciturn man would resist; then, at a nod from Cady, he relinquished his package.

There was dead silence while Rafe scanned the contents, then walked to the portable tape recorder, snapped in the cassette, and switched the machine on.

Bruno's and Todd's voices were quite clear. Though their words were terse, the meaning was obvious. At the end of the tape, Rafe stared at Trock, then at Cady, his hand fondling the Doberman's head. The pit bull terrier lay quietly at Cady's feet, watching. "I'm not as surprised as you might think, Cady. I've been suspicious of Bruno for quite some time now," he said. Rafe spoke in a relaxed way. He leaned down and took a pencil-slim cheroot from a silver box on the table, then asked Trock if he would like some coffee. The man shook his head.

"There were pictures." Cady bit her lip. "They were going to use them to make me force you to help destroy the environmental bill and other bills that didn't suit them." Her voice had a grainy sound.

"They?" Rafe looked at her through the curl of smoke.

"Bruno . . . Todd Leacock . . . I suppose Greeley . . ." She sipped the scalding coffee, ignoring the way it burned her throat.

Rafe rolled the cigar between his fingers, then looked at Trock. "Continue what you're doing, but now report back to me as well as to my wife." The man nodded once and left. Rafe tapped the ash from his cheroot. "I take it that the pictures were bad." He sat down facing her again.

"Horrible," Cady choked. "More came today." She set the cup onto the saucer with a clatter.

Rafe stared at her for long moments. "Get them."

"No."

"Cady, get the pictures."

Feeling catatonic, she rose, went to the file cabinet, unlocked it, took out the two boxes, and held them in her hands. She stared at them, knowing her life was over, that she would go on breathing but she would really be dead.

Rafe was there to lead her back to her chair and push her gently down into it, then remove the boxes from her grasp. He opened them, perused the pictures in both boxes slowly, then replaced the tops and put the boxes on the floor at his feet.

Cady kept her eyes on his face, even though she knew her own was bright red and her insides on fire.

Rafe looked up at her. "That woman has a rather good body, but it isn't quite as good as yours. The photographer should have been more thorough and gotten a woman with a crescent mole under her left nipple." Rafe still looked at her. The muscle under his eye jumped once.

Hope blossomed in Cady. "Rob said I should wait to tell you, that maybe we could take care of it without upsetting you with this whole sordid business."

"You told *him?* You showed him these pictures?" Rafe's features seemed set in concrete.

Cady felt his anger radiate around the room. "Yes. I called him . . . because . . . because I was afraid." How could she tell Rafe of her paralyzing fear of losing him?

"Isn't that what a husband is for?" Rafe spat out the words as though they were poison in his mouth.

"Yes." Misery coursed through Cady.

Rafe took a deep breath. "I'm going to kill Bruno and that Leacock for putting you through this." His voice was so matter-of-fact that Cady was sure she must have misheard him.

Before she could reply, the buzzer on the phone sounded twice, signaling that the call was for her. She lifted the receiver and Rob spoke to her. "Rob, listen"— Cady gulped a breath—"I just talked to Rafe. He knows all about it." Cady looked at her husband as he gestured that he wanted the phone. "Just a moment, Rob."

Cady listened through a fog as the men talked. She was aware that Rafe was talking to Rob about the necessity of getting information on Bruno. All at once she remembered what Stacy had given her at lunch the day they met. She looked at Rafe, then rose to her feet and went to the filing cabinet, knowing that his eyes were on her every moment. She held the envelope on her lap until Rafe had replaced the receiver, then she handed it to him in silence.

He opened the manila package, lifted the thin pile of papers, and began reading.

Cady watched, agonized, as his color fluctuated from pale gray to brick red. When he finished, his clenching hands threatened to destroy the papers altogether. Cady bit her lip, not interfering.

All at once Rafe seemed to realize what he was doing. His long fingers pressed the papers smooth. "Well, Cady, I guess you've realized what a fool your husband was . . . is. You said you wouldn't get rid of me until I was three kinds of a jackass. I guess now is the time."

"Are you going to divorce me because of the pictures? They could ruin your career," Cady ventured, feeling shy with him.

"God, no, I'm not going to allow you even to be touched by them. They couldn't wreck my career, Cady. I intend to bring this out in the open and expose Greeley and Trabold and that sleazy louse Leacock. You have nothing to be ashamed of, my love," Rafe said, his face a mask of anger. "No one is going to get away with intimidating you. I promise you that."

"Rafe—" Before she could speak, the phone rang again. This time it was for Rafe.

Cady had the feeling he would be on the phone a long time. Feeling tired and wrung out, she mouthed to Rafe that she was going to bed.

She didn't even bother to shower, settling for a sponge bath and then falling into a druglike sleep.

The next day she struggled awake as though she were fighting her way through miles of black velvet. Her eyes seemed to be glued shut.

"Open your eyes, darling," Rafe whispered. "I have juice for you. Ice-cold orange juice, just the way you like it."

Cady unstuck her eyes, feeling her stomach rise into her throat as Rafe sat down on the edge of the bed and proffered the glass. "Take it away," she said faintly, locking her mouth as she began to gag. "Ohhhh, Rafe, move."

Rafe stared at her as she tried to push him away. Then he placed the glass on the table and swung her out of the bed in one motion, striding to the bathroom as he wrapped her in a robe.

"Put me down. I'm sick," Cady groaned.

"There you are, sweetheart," Rafe crooned, holding her head as she retched.

When she was finished, Rafe stripped off the sweat-soaked robe he had wrapped her in and set her gently in the tub, cushioning her head on the bath pillow, then slipping in beside her to hold her while the tub filled with warm water.

"Were you going to tell me you were pregnant soon, or were you just going to wait and let me notice your figure rounding out?" He smiled down at her, wiping her face with a soft cloth.

"I feel green," Cady moaned, weak and grateful for the muscular body supporting hers. "How did you get out of your clothes so fast?" she asked dully.

"Practice," Rafe soothed, washing her body, his touch gentle.

"Thank you." Cady spoke into his neck.

"For what, love?" Rafe's lips feathered her cheek.

"For taking care of me."

"That's my primary mission in life. Didn't you know that?"

"Nice," Cady muttered as he lifted her, dried her, then carried her back to bed. "I can get up now, Rafe. Really. I'll get dressed and eat breakfast with you."

"No." He left the room in a run.

Before Cady could feel too sorry for herself for being abandoned, Rafe was back, a bed tray in his hands. He grinned at her. Right behind him came Mrs. Lacey with a teapot and a platter of toasted muffins on a tray, and a large jug of orange juice. "I can't eat all that." Cady stared at the tray Rafe set across her lap.

Then Mrs. Lacey brought a table close to the bed and set her things on that. "You mustn't mind the morning sickness, ma'am. It will soon pass." She smiled at them, then closed the door behind her.

Rafe removed his robe and slipped into bed beside her. "You're not going to eat it all. Some of it's for me, love." He kissed her nose, then poured her some fresh juice.

"What about the glass there?" Cady pointed to the juice Rafe had placed on the bedside table when he had taken Cady to the bathroom.

He shrugged. "I'll drink it. After all, we'll be here for a while."

"You have to go to your office." Cady sipped the icy juice, grateful for her settling stomach.

"Nope. I called and said I wouldn't be in today." He grinned at her and tapped his glass against hers. "Nothing so major that it couldn't be put off." He spread raspberry jam on a toasted muffin and fed it to her. He laughed because he had gotten jam on her nose, and leaned down to lick it off. Cady felt her heart flutter like a bird's wings in her chest. If only they could always be so close. "If you don't feel like going to my father's Christmas bash, you don't have to," he offered.

"I *want* to go. I want to be there when you expose Bruno and Greeley." She cuddled close to her husband, savoring the feel of his arm around her shoulders as he fed her more of the muffin. "I still don't see how you're going to get Todd there."

"I had Stacy call him and say that Bruno wants him there to take pictures. Since Bruno is in New York on a job for Emmett, it was easy. If Emmett hadn't sent Bruno on that errand, I would have dreamed up some other reason for him to be out of town until just before the party. Unless something goes radically wrong, Leacock should show up just about the time Bruno and Greeley are beginning to feel comfortable."

"Aren't you afraid that Bruno will allow the pictures to be made public?" Cady shivered.

Rafe folded her closer to his body, pressing a kiss to the top of her head. "You keep forgetting to trust your husband." He caressed her ear with his lips. "A few of my staff and I contacted some other legislators and informed them of what we're up against. When we told them we hoped to get wives of other politicians to let us use their heads to superimpose on the body that's under your head in the photographs Leacock sent you, we were buried in volunteers." He looked down into her aghast face. "I'm not kidding you. We had too many women to use, so we used the most prominent. If Bruno decides to print the pictures he has, then we'll release our pictures and prove what a fraud they are. In fact, Jack Van Orden says that his wife and some of the others feel that we should publicize ours anyway, sort of taking the team out of any plans Bruno may have in the future. I haven't made up my mind what I'll do yet. I want to talk to all the wives first."

"I don't believe this is happening!" Cady gulped. "You mean the nightmare is over?"

"Almost. We deliver the coup de grace at Durra, at the Christmas party. I'm sure Emmett won't be pleased when he discovers just how crooked his protégé is," Rafe grated, his hands clenching on her.

"Your sisters will be furious for exposing him at Durra." Cady shuddered.

Rafe's laughter rumbled under her cheek. "My sisters will be quiet—or their husbands will tell them to shut up. I've talked to both my brothers-in-law, and they're cooperating with me."

"Oh, Rafe, I can't believe it. I feel as though someone has lifted a cement block off my chest." She sighed, happiness making her bold as she kissed his bare chest.

"Cady, love, don't do that," he mumbled into her hair. "I can't make love to you, so . . ."

Cady leaned back until she was looking up at him. "Who told you that fairy tale? My doctor says that all normal activity is acceptable. I don't think I should take up sky diving, but . . ." She wriggled against him, liking the feel of his taut flesh against her.

"Am I to take it, Mrs. Densmore, that you consider lovemaking normal activity?" Rafe's mouth slid down her body, then up to her neck.

"Well, it sure beats jogging," Cady breathed in gasping amusement.

Rafe stroked her, then leaned over to kiss her abdomen. "I should hope so." He stared at the point where his mouth had been. "It's going to be a little honey-haired girl with violet eyes. I know it. God, she'll be beautiful."

"The doctor didn't say anything about twins, and since I have ordered a little boy with hair the color of dark chocolate . . ."

"Girl." Rafe fastened his mouth to her breast and her protest became a moan. "Cady, darling, did I tell you that you are more beautiful ill than any other woman in the world is at her best? I can't wait to see you as your pregnancy progresses."

"You'll hate me," Cady wailed, feeling lightheaded at his words. "I'll look like a balloon."

"You'll be perfect." Since Rafe proceeded to show Cady just exactly how perfect he seemed to think her, her wails turned to delighted sighs.

Their loveplay increased until all that could be heard were the whispered sighs of satisfaction. Cady had a feeling that she had just skied down a ninety-degree incline, then floated back to the top.

"Rafe . . . Rafe, does everyone feel this way?" she muttered, her fingers digging into his shoulders.

His words were lost in her body as they rose together in a spiral of love.

Not once but many times, Rafe brought her to that pinnacle of joy that she knew could only happen with him. He was her love, the very core of her happiness.

"We're lucky," Cady murmured to her husband as she let her hands wander over his body, giggling when she felt a tautened response to her touch.

Rafe nuzzled her abdomen, his tongue teasing her navel. "No one should have the power over another human being that you have over me," he growled softly into her willing flesh, laughing gently when her body responded to the most intimate kiss.

Over and over they ministered to each other with a gentle, powerful passion that swept away all the rough edges of misunderstanding.

"Are we really going to stay in bed all day?" Cady yawned in the aftermath of their love, then poked Rafe in the ribs when he shouted with laughter.

"I think we'd better. I'm wearing you out."

"Not so. I'm wearing you out." She tried to rise.

"We'll get up on one condition. That we go down and swim in the pool, take a sauna, then rest again."

Cady stared up at his laughing face, his body resting on his elbows. "Then it will be dinnertime." She chuckled.

At once Rafe was serious. "That's the most natural laugh I've heard from you in days." He leaned down to run his lips along her jaw. "I love hearing you laugh, seeing you relax." He reached for her, lifting her out of bed, then carrying her to the closet while he selected a terry-cloth robe for her. "I fully intend that you shall have the most relaxed pregnancy in the world."

"For our first, you mean?" Cady allowed herself to be dressed in the robe, feeling lazy as she watched him tie the belt at her waist.

His head jerked up at her words. "Oh? Are we having more?" The gleam in his eye made her redden.

"It seems like a good idea." She wanted to yell at him that she wanted ten children that looked just like him, but even if they had none, she wanted to be with him.

"I agree." He left her for a moment, then came back with a toga around his waist.

"You forgot our bathing suits, Rafe." Cady grinned at him.

"No, I didn't." His grin had that impish look. "We won't be using any."

"We can't!" Cady let him pull her down the hall to the back staircase. "What if Mrs. Lacey or Trock comes into the pool area?" She was whispering as they entered the large kitchen.

"Mrs. Lacey, we don't wish to be disturbed in the pool," Rafe informed the housekeeper, a smile on his face. "No calls, no visitors. Save everything until I come to tell you that I'm ready to take calls again."

Cady squirmed as the housekeeper nodded and smiled. "Time you two had some moments to yourselves." Mrs. Lacey nodded once, then turned back to the silver she had spread on the table in front of her, the polishing cloth in her hand.

The pool area had a damp, hollow-sounding atmosphere with the bubble spread over it. Cady had the feeling that she and Rafe were the only two people on earth.

They played like children for over an hour. Then they sat in the sauna for a short time. Finally Rafe insisted on giving her a massage. Cady felt cosseted and loved.

The word mushroomed in her mind after their shower as she watched her husband dry her with a fluffy towel. Did he love her? If he didn't, he was giving a very good imitation of it. All that remained was for him to say the words she longed to hear: "I love you, Cady."

That night they dined on broiled crab. Mrs. Lacey listened patiently to Rafe as he pointed out how important it was for Cady to have nutritious meals.

Cady looked from one to the other, bemused, as they discoursed on the efficacy of fruit with every meal and vegetables cooked al dente.

Rafe looked over at her and clucked. "Darling, you have butter on your chin." He dabbed at the melted butter, then kissed her in front of the indulgently smiling Mrs. Lacey.

The days passed in a euphoric wonder that awed Cady. She didn't seem able to stop smiling. She spent many happy hours Christmas shopping as the season advanced and the morning sickness receded.

When the day dawned for Emmett's Christmas party, Cady's nervousness had been considerably mitigated by Rafe's attentiveness and his obvious enthusiasm for the coming confrontation at Durra.

She was deciding what she would wear when Mrs. Lacey buzzed to say that Cady's brothers-in law were waiting for her in the library.

Throwing on a pair of faded jeans and a roll-neck sweater, she strolled into the library and grinned at the twins. "So what bank did you—" Cady stopped in mid-sentence on seeing the unaccustomed sobriety on the twins' faces. For once it wasn't Gareth who jumped into the conversation.

"Cady, didn't you say that your father was coming in for Emmett's party?" Gavin was grim-faced.

Cady sat down and gestured to the twins to sit. Gavin did. Gareth prowled the library. "I think you'd better tell me what's wrong and what my father has to do with it."

Gavin leaned forward, rubbing his hands on his knees. "Your father has nothing to do with it, Cady. We just thought he might help us." He swallowed. "Some guy by the name of Todd Leacock says he has proof that Gareth tried to shave points in the Cornell–Notre Dame game." Gavin watched her like a cat watching goldfish.

"It's a lie," Cady said, watching as the prowling Gareth spun to stare at her, a misty look in his eyes.

"How do you know?" Gareth's voice was hoarse.

"Two ways." Cady smiled at him. "I know you. You're a brat at times, but you're honest." She stopped smiling. "And I know Todd Leacock. He's a heel who works for Bruno Trabold." She gave them a hard look. "You must have tweaked Bruno's tail once too often." At the murderous expressions that came over the twins' faces, she held up her hand palm outward. "Whoa. Don't get up a head of steam. Rafe is taking care of it. If you behave, I'll fill you in on the master plan. Dave and Harrison are already in on it." She smiled, urging them to sit down again. "It looks as though this will be a family affair."

By the time she was finished sketching the machinations of Bruno Trabold and being firm about refusing to show the twins the pictures, it was lunchtime. Cady had no trouble persuading the boys to stay.

As she passed them the platter of cold chicken and roast beef and the loaf-size rolls that Mrs. Lacey had made, the twins were relaxed and smiling. "Now tell me how you planned to involve my poor father in all this," Cady requested.

Gavin swallowed and took a drink of milk. "Well, he's been at the university for years. He would know about these things. We thought he could give us some advice."

Cady laughed. "About point shaving?" She shrugged. "I'm not sure he would know much about it, but I think he'd have put you on the right track. He would probably have sent you to Rafe."

"Or to you." Gareth saluted her with his glass of milk. "We knew you'd help us, Cady. You have so much courage—you're not afraid of anything."

The admiring glances turned her way made Cady glow inside. "I'm no heroine." Her smile widened. "Even though being married to Rafe has taught me what courage is."

"That's what he says about you." Gavin smiled at her.

"He does?"

"C'mon, Cady, you know how Rafe dotes on you," Gareth scoffed. "When he first met you, he acted like a guy who'd just had a lobotomy." He laughed loudly. "Remember, Gavin? He had just bought the Porsche and he would never let anyone near it. Then one day after he met Cady, you and I were over at his apartment in Georgetown admiring it. When I said—just joking, of course—that it would be nice to borrow the car for the evening, Rafe just gave me a glazed look and said, 'Sure, go ahead.'" Gareth threw back his head and laughed harder.

"I remember," Gavin said. "I asked him if he had lost his mind and he mumbled, 'No, my heart.' Then his face turned beet red and he walked back into his apartment."

"Did he really do that?" Cady asked dreamily, her chin in her hands.

Gareth scowled at her. "Damn it, Cady, don't be such a baby doll. You led Rafe around by the nose and he loved it."

"No!"

"Yes," the twins chorused.

Later, when they rose to go, they both kissed Cady on the cheek and told her to wear her prettiest dress that night.

"Always dress well for a hanging, Cady." Gareth gave her a look so much like Rafe's mischievous expression that she caught her breath.

That evening before Rafe arrived home, she was in the tub soaking in an exotic essence he had brought her from India, where he'd gone on a fact-finding trip. Unlike many of his political colleagues, Rafe had paid his own way and not charged the trip to the taxpayers. At the time there had been a decided coolness between him and Cady, and though he had given her a perfunctory invitation to join him, she had felt that he didn't really want her to come.

She stood in her terry-cloth robe, a damp towel arranged like a turban around her hair to keep it wet while the conditioner worked. Though she scrutinized each formal dress she owned, in her own mind there was no doubt what she would wear that evening—even though her prudent self told her to forget it.

She pulled the chocolate-brown sheath from the closet and held it up in front of her. It was watered silk, strapless, with a matching stole in the same fabric. There were tiny, deep violet flowers sewn at the breast and along the top of the deep ruffle that edged the hem. Each of the small violet flowers had tiny brown hearts in the center. The dress was dramatic and had nothing to do with Christmas. But Emmett had an unwritten rule that the women who attended his Christmas soirees wear either green or red. The decorations at Durra would echo those colors.

Cady rubbed her body with perfumed lotion prior to donning the brown bikini panties that were the only garment she would wear under the figure-hugging silk. Her hair was left bouncing clean and fresh on her bare shoulders. Deeming the dress too modern to coordinate with her antique amethysts, she decided to leave her ears bare. She chose to wear a thin gold chain around her neck as her only adornment. She would take the stole even though she knew that Emmett kept the house quite hot. Emmett thought that energy conservation was for other people to worry about.

She was turning to look at her back in the three-way mirror when Rafe entered from the connecting bathroom, his shirt studs still undone, two boxes in his hands.

"I called Mrs. Lacey to see what dresses you had put out to decide among for tonight." He grinned at her. "When she mentioned that one of the dresses was neither green nor red, I took a chance you might pick it. Rebel." He handed her the larger of the two boxes.

As Cady lifted the cluster of tiny purple orchids from the box, she oohed her delight.

Rafe let his eyes rove over her in slow appreciation. "Where will you pin them, love? It seems there's a great deal of you showing." He let his forefinger trace the low-cut neckline, lingering with obvious pleasure on her creamy skin. "You're so very beautiful."

"I'll pin them at my waist," Cady breathed, feeling giddy because of the look in his eyes.

"Will you?" he drawled, his finger gentle in the valley between her breasts. "I'd rather stay home altogether and discuss where the flowers should go."

"You would?" Cady swayed toward him, then paused, sighing. "We can't. Your father will be expecting us, and my father will be here soon as well."

Rafe snapped his fingers. "That's what I wanted to tell you." He leaned forward and kissed her nose. "You're too distracting. Your father is here now. I knew what time his plane was coming in, so I picked him up on the way home. He's changing now."

"Rafe," Cady chided him as he rained butterfly kisses on her cheek, "you should have told me at once."

"Yes," he muttered, his attention seeming fixed on her ear. Then he jerked back from her. "That's the other thing I wanted to show you." He lifted his hand to caress her hair. "I didn't remember you having jewelry for this dress, soooo—I called Cartier's today . . ." He grinned like a boy as he popped open the other box in front of her.

Cady stared at the drop earrings that looked like braid—braid made up of amethysts. There was also a braided necklace of the same amethysts. She reached up to remove the gold chain, but Rafe's hands were there before hers. He fastened the necklace, then stood back to let her insert the pierced earrings. She looked at herself, then at the image of Rafe peering over her shoulder. "I love them."

"They match your eyes . . . but they aren't as pretty." Rafe slipped his hands around her and pressed his lips to her neck. He let out a gusty breath. "I suppose we have to go this evening, but I tell you now, love, if it weren't for pulling the rug out from under Bruno, we'd be staying home, even with your father here and invited to his party."

"Aye, aye, sir," Cady said with a mock salute.

"Brat." Rafe swatted her backside, then strode toward his own room, calling behind him to Cady to check if there was ice to make her father a drink before they left for Durra.

Trock had seen to the ice and had already handed Professor Nesbitt a glass of wine when Cady entered the room. She smiled as her father talked to the two dogs that lay sprawled at his feet.

"What do you think of those two now?" Cady walked into her father's arms.

"You'd never recognize either of them from the rag-and-bone condition they were once in." The professor sipped his wine, then nodded his thanks to Trock, who turned at once to fix a glass of mineral water for Cady.

"Trock." Rafe strode into the room, looking vital, strong, and very handsome, Cady thought. "I want you to accompany us this evening and bring the dogs," Rafe said calmly, making his father-in-law's brows arch and his wife gasp.

"You can't," Cady pointed out. "Emmett hates dogs. So does Bruno."

Rafe grinned at her. "So they do. And so does Greeley."

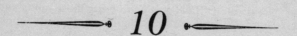

10

DURRA WAS A Christmas fairyland of green and red. Green and red lights festooned the trees, the hedges, the colonnades, the windows. A huge spruce at the curve of the drive was draped in green and white with red. The rest of the decorations were all red and green.

"You'll be the belle of the ball, my love," Rafe whispered to Cady as she hesitated on the fan-shape steps leading to the front door.

"I'll stick out like a sore thumb," Cady gulped, glad of his hand at her back as they stepped into the foyer, which was also ablaze with green and red. Her father stepped forward first and shook Emmett's hand. He bent over Lee Terris's hand in a courtly manner. If he looked surprised at the effusive welcome the twins gave him, he quickly masked it.

"That's something I have to tell you, later," Cady muttered to Rafe. "Bruno and the twins."

Rafe nodded, his face grim.

Then Emmett was looking at Cady, his eyes widening

in shock. Before he could speak, Cady grasped his hand, shook it, said, "Nice to be here," and turned to Lee Terris. Emmett was still looking at her, open-mouthed, as his son wrung his limp hand.

"My dear Cady." Lee looked pained. "Has no one ever told you that we wear green and red at Durra?" She was dressed in red velvet.

"Has no one ever told you that being repetitive is dull?" Cady retorted. She gave Lee a wide smile and patted her on the arm, then moved toward the twins, who were grinning at the red-faced Lee.

When Cady heard Emmett bellow behind her, she braced herself and turned slowly.

"No, damn it, Rafe, you can't bring those mutts into this house. And what's *he* doing here?" Emmett fulminated, the angry red of his face fitting right in with the decorations. "What? What surprise are you talking about? What do you mean I'll understand later?" He glowered at his eldest son. "I don't like it. You'd better make sure neither of those mutts chews up my guests." He threw an angry glance Cady's way, then glared at the placid animals who were sitting on either side of Trock as he stood behind Rafe.

Since the long guest list for the Durra Christmas get-together made it more a mob scene than a party, Emmett was soon distracted from the dogs. A ten-piece band provided music, though most of the guests would wait until after dinner to dance. Still, a few couples had eschewed cocktails and were on the solarium floor swaying to the big-band sound.

"Shall we, Mrs. Densmore?" Rafe kissed her ear.

"I thought you would want to talk to some of your—" Cady was delighted when Rafe interrupted her by sweeping her onto the dance floor. Her heart was fluttering wildly when he began to sing the words to "Everything I Have Is Yours" into her ear, his sure baritone caressing and deep.

"I like it when you sing to me, Rafe." She leaned

back to look up into his face.

"Do you, angel?" His eyes roved over her. "I like it when you do anything to me...except ignore me, of course." He pressed her closer. "Did I tell you that you're the most beautiful woman here?" He swung her away from his body as the tempo changed, then brought her back, dipped her, and swung her away again.

Breathless, Cady laughed up at him. "I never ignore you."

Rafe nodded, then caught her close to him again, concern etched deep on his face. "I forgot for a moment. Is it all right for you to dance fast like this?"

"Of course it is." Cady twirled around him. "Dancing is good exercise."

"Don't you whirl like that again. Your legs showed clear up to the thighs," Rafe growled, catching her close as the music died.

Dinner was a noisy gathering of round tables of ten each that filled the ballroom to overflowing. The centerpieces were spruce greens and red carnations. Some tables had red candles; others had green. Cady was seated at a table with Rob Ardmore. At a nearby table sat Todd Leacock, his smile knowing when he caught her eye. It was all Cady could do to keep a bland look on her face.

"That's Leacock." Cady smiled at Rob as though she were telling him a joke. "The one with the cranberry-color dinner clothes."

Rob smiled and lifted his glass to her to acknowledge that he knew whom she meant. "Bruno isn't here yet." Rob's smile widened. "I sure hope he gets here soon."

"He will." Cady's voice held more confidence than she felt. She had a shivery feeling that Bruno had somehow discovered their plans and was at that very moment winging his way to Katmandu.

Later Cady sipped her after-dinner Cointreau and listened to Emmett relate how well the merger between Densmore Ltd., a British affiliate, and Werrings Electronics had gone, that profits were up at every quarter.

Cady couldn't help but think her father-in-law looked like one of the strutting peacocks that roamed the front lawn at Durra. She had to fight back a laugh as his friend Greeley wiped crumbs from his portly front and announced that he, too, was proud of his efforts in the past year. Much of the legislation that his group of lobbyists had backed had been pushed through Congress.

"Great country, America." Greeley belched delicately.

Cady could feel Rafe looking her way, but she knew that if she looked at him she would laugh out loud.

Feeling more at ease now, Cady was not prepared for Bruno's entrance into the room. One moment she was sipping her liqueur and listening to Gavin talk about a course that was giving him trouble, then she looked up, choking on the hot, sweet liquid. Bruno! As he stood in the doorway leading to the hall, to Cady he looked like a vulture in a tuxedo.

She took a deep breath and glanced from Bruno to Todd, realizing at once that Bruno hadn't seen his cohort.

"Take a seat, Bruno," Emmett roared, flapping his hand to bring the man forward.

Bruno relaxed against the doorjamb. "I won't bother, since you seem to be through." He straightened from the door and left, presumably for the solarium.

Cady exhaled a shuddering sigh, not aware until that moment that she had been holding her breath.

As the diners rose and separated into chatting groups that moved leisurely toward the solarium and the music, Cady stretched her neck to watch Rafe. He winked at her but made no attempt to join her. He was smiling and seeming to maneuver several people, including his father, toward the library. Aveen and Aileen, as their father's hostesses, had gone immediately to the solarium.

"I think the time is near," Rob said in a mock-sepulchral tone.

Cady could sense his excitement.

The twins were waiting in the doorway leading from the ballroom as Cady and Rob approached.

"Rafe said to come to the library." Gavin leaned down toward her and added in a whisper, "Gareth is bringing Leacock last. Leacock thinks he's meeting Bruno there."

As Gavin pushed open the door, Cady could hear Emmett growling at Rafe that he had to get back to his guests. Then, as Cady and the twins stepped through the door, Bruno's eyes fixed on them, narrowing. He was standing with Emmett, a bored-looking Lee Terris next to him.

When Trock walked through the door with the dogs, Bruno's face had a ferret cast to it. Cady had the feeling that he had penetrated every mind in the room and sniffed out danger to himself. When she saw him turn in a casual way toward the double doors leading from the library to the terrace, she turned to tell Trock.

Trock had already whispered a command to the Doberman, who needed no urging. Graf flung himself at Bruno, taking a growling stance between the doors and the man.

"What the hell . . ." Bruno snarled. "Get this dog out of here. Emmett, are you going to let this beast—"

"Rafe," Emmett roared, "what did I say about those dogs?"

"Simmer down, Dad. Graf is only following orders. *My orders.*" Rafe's voice was bland, but there was a hard glitter in his eyes as he turned to Cady, then watched as the door opened and Gareth almost pushed Todd Leacock through it, followed him, and closed and locked it behind him. Todd's face was a hunted mask as he watched Trabold's face.

"Now I think we're all here." Rafe looked around the room, giving a grim smile to his fellow legislators and their wives and husbands, who were clustered near the Adams fireplace.

"Actually, not all the people who volunteered to get involved in our little experiment are here," Rafe announced. "There were too many volunteers, but I think most of you recognize Senator Jack Van Orden and his wife, Senator Bill Darien and his wife, Congresswoman

Gilda Reeves and her husband, Senator Mary Lake and her husband and, of course, Congressman Rob Ardmore. I have a list of many others who—"

"Rafe, what the hell are we doing here?" Emmett bellowed.

"I'm getting to that, Dad. First I want you all to see some pictures. Gavin, bring over that corkboard standing in the corner." Rafe smiled at the assembly. "Gavin managed to sneak this into the library for me this evening."

Graf growled as Bruno tried to move. When Todd Leacock sidled toward the door, Trock whispered to the pit bull, who at once stood spread-legged in front of Leacock. The dog's mouth was open in a snarling threat.

When the board was turned toward the assembled group, there were gasps, groans, hisses, imprecations.

Cady closed her eyes, unable to look at herself in that promiscuous pose, even though the other wives and female legislators were on the board with her. She clenched her fists and opened her eyes.

"Really, Cady, you might have considered the family name." Lee stepped closer to Emmett.

"Shut up, Lee," Rafe said lightly, his voice friendly but his eyes agate-hard. "What you're seeing is an abortive attempt at blackmail. An attempt by—well, let's just say, for the moment, very criminal-type people to put pressure on my wife, who would, in turn, put pressure on me to pull my support away from an environmental bill that would help my state and the country." Rafe turned to Gareth. "Bring Greeley in here, along with Dave and Harrison. If Aileen and Aveen want to come, let them. Tell them to let Cousin Michaeline play hostess."

"She'd love that," Gareth said cheekily before closing the door behind him.

Emmett was red-faced and pop-eyed as his graze traveled from the pictures to Cady to Rafe to the other women to Rob Ardmore. "Why are you calling Greeley?" he demanded. "He would have none of such stuff."

"But you do see what a phony setup this is?" Rafe

took a cheroot from his gold case and lit it. Then he looked at Professor Nesbitt, who stood off to one side, stony-faced and silent. "Only you and I, sir, would know that a picture of Cady would have to include her most interesting mole."

"Rafe!" Cady exclaimed, mortified. She wasn't placated when her father chuckled.

"Sorry, darling." Rafe's smile was tender.

A sudden silence filled the room, so that the rather hoarse breathing of Todd Leacock was abrasive to the ears.

Greeley came through the door, his bald pate having a pinkish sheen in the red and green decorative lights from the foyer. The cigar in his mouth flapped up and down as he looked at the people in the library. His button eyes, lost in the folds of fat on his cheeks, stared from Emmett to Bruno. It was Gareth's ungentle urging that propelled him into the center of the room after his shifting eyes found the corkboard with its interesting array of pictures.

"I want to talk to my lawyer," Greeley snarled, glaring at Bruno. "I didn't want any part of this, Rafe. It was that damn fool who thought he could sink you."

Bruno snarled and turned toward the door. At once the Doberman rose to attack. Rafe yelled at the dog and threw himself forward at the same time. "Back, Graf. I want him for myself."

When Bruno heard this, he turned around and launched himself at Rafe. It seemed to Cady that they met in midair.

She stood there, mute. The snarling, whining dogs, prevented from helping their beloved master, quivered with frustration. Emmett yelped when a small table with some of his precious Belleek china crashed to the floor. Lee Terris moved to get some of the other precious artifacts out of the way. Cady was frozen to the spot. She wanted to kill Rob Ardmore when he urged Rafe to "Let him have it with a left." Rafe, be careful, she screamed in her mind.

The noise increased as the twins egged their older brother on to the kill. Gareth stood close to Leacock, telling Hobo what a good boy he was for watching the "bad man." Hobo only snarled.

Cady felt fright and anger when Rafe's fellow legislators and his twin brothers formed a loosely knit ring around the fighting men. For a moment Cady couldn't see, even stretching her neck and standing on tiptoe. Finally she stepped onto one of Emmett's fine needle-pointed Sheraton chairs. Graf whined at her feet.

What Cady saw made her knees turn to jelly. "Father, stop them, stop them!" Cady was sure her father couldn't even hear her hoarse whisper.

All at once the fight was over. Rafe was standing there swaying, the back of one hand dabbing at the corner of his mouth.

Cady jumped down from the chair and pushed her way through the knot of men just as Jack Van Orden hoisted Bruno to his feet.

For a moment Cady paused, then she catapulted herself onto Rafe. "Did he hurt you? Did he hurt you?" She ran her fingers over the swelling under his left eye, not even trying to check the tears coursing down her cheeks. "Oh, Rafe, your poor face." She slipped her hands around his waist, cradling him to her. "That monster marked your cheek," Cady railed, turning in front of him to glare at the staggering Bruno. "You—you—louse." Cady lifted her hands like claws, feeling anger fill her veins. Before she could move, two arms clamped around her waist.

"Easy, darling," Rafe muttered into her hair. "The fighting is over for today . . . and I feel so damn good."

Cady looked up at him. He was glowering at Bruno. "Rafe, Bruno tried to blackmail the twins, too," she told him. "He accused Gareth of shaving points in a game. It's a lie. Todd was in on it, too."

Emmett's angry roar drowned out Rafe's answer. "You viper! Try to destroy my boys, will you? I'll have you put away for a thousand years."

* * *

By the time Bruno and Todd had been led away by the security people that Emmett employed, Aileen and Aveen, who had come to the library to see what was keeping their father from his guests, had a fair idea of what had taken place. White-faced, they stared at Bruno as he walked past them.

"We trusted you," Aileen accused. Aveen nodded in agreement.

"Which shows how foolish even you can be at times, darling," Dave said mildly, putting an arm around his wife.

Aileen swallowed and nodded. "In more ways than one." She leaned against her husband, her eyes misty.

"I never expected Cady to be such a ruffian," Aveen mumbled to her husband.

"Don't be a fool. She's more a lady than anyone I know...except you, of course." Harrison squeezed her hand, but Aveen's smile was shaky.

"Aveen and Aileen have just passed through a belated puberty of the soul," Gavin whispered to Cady. "Maybe now their spiritual growth will pull even with the ego growth—they might mature."

Emmett began ushering his guests out of the library, vowing to each one to see to it that Bruno and his cohorts were punished.

Gavin grinned at Cady. "One by one, you've turned the Densmores into humans, Cady dear. Now if you'll find me a girl just like you, I'll be content for life."

"Me, too," Gareth said, lifting Cady high in the air.

"Hey, be careful with her." Rafe was there, taking Cady out of Gareth's arms into his own. He held her against his chest, chuckling at her flustered look. "She's going to have a baby. I don't want her handled roughly."

The twins whooped, making Emmett, who was standing at the library door with Lee Terris, turn and glower at them. Dave and Harrison kissed Cady. Aileen and Aveen kissed Rafe. Rafe kissed Cady and didn't release her. Still, he managed to shake hands all around. Thomas Nesbitt watched his daughter, a contented smile on his face.

Cady was sure that Rafe would be worn out and she suggested that they leave rather then go back to the solarium and dance.

"Not on your life, my love. I'm celebrating. The only reason I'll leave is if you tell me you're tired. Then I'll go." His face seemed to have an aura all its own as he looked at her. "Aveen said she would mend the tear in my jacket. Aileen put peroxide on my face. Now I want to waltz with my beautiful wife and discuss a trip to Santo Tomas the day after Christmas . . . just the two of us."

"I'd love to dance for a while." Cady glowed at the look in her husband's eyes. "As for Santo Tomas, it can't come too soon for me." She swallowed and looked deep into his eyes as he swept her onto the floor to the waltz music that Emmett was so addicted to. "The best Christmas present I could ever have would be to have you all to myself. You see, I love you so much, I can't see straight." She gulped a laugh as Rafe stopped dead in the middle of the dance floor.

"Do you mean it?" His voice had the roughness of velvet rubbed the wrong way. The bones in his face seemed to crack, spread, and mend in different places as he struggled with the words she had spoken to him. "Cady, my God, you do choose your times!" His voice seemed forced from his throat. "What do you think my father would say if I picked you up in my arms and ran out the door with you?" He was trying to be flip, but Cady could see the blue flame leaping in his eyes as he watched her. He began dancing with her again, his body bent over her in a protective bow.

When the tempo changed to a rock and roll beat, Emmett was not the only one who frowned. Rafe's face creased with concern as Cady swung away from him, her body gyrating in delighted concert with the music.

"What's the matter, big brother?" Gareth jibed, dancing close to them, a curvy brunette dancing opposite him. "If you can't hack it, *I'll* dance with Cady."

"The hell you will," Rafe said, smiling at his brother and at once moving with his wife to the music. "Are you sure it's all right, love?" His eyes couldn't seem to stop roving over her body.

Cady felt alive, light as air, and as beautiful as Cinderella because Rafe was looking at her like that. If only he would just tell her he loved her, life would be absolutely perfect.

The day after Christmas they flew to Santo Tomas Island. Rafe left firm instructions that he was not to be disturbed unless it was a state of national emergency.

Cady stared at her slightly rounded belly protruding over the bikini bottom and poked her tongue at the mirror image.

Rafe came into the room in the briefest silky trunks. "My God, woman, you drive me wild with desire."

Cady stared at him, open-mouthed, thinking he was mocking her, when she became aware of the arousal he took no pains to hide.

He grinned at her. "What's it going to be like when I'm ninety and I have to explain to our great-grandchildren how their great-grandmother still arouses me? Aren't you ashamed to have such power over me?"

"No." She opened her arms to him as he lifted her and carried her out to the beach. "You're always carrying me," she muttered into his ear. "Are you positive it's safe?"

"Yes. I can't seem to keep my hands off you." Rafe gave her a rueful grin as he set her on the blanket he had spread out on the white sand. His eyes held a wicked gleam. "What say we swim nude, lady?"

Cady looked around her at the empty beach and water. "We can't. Can we?"

"Sure we can. There's no one around, wife of mine."

"You won't think I'm awful to look at?" she ventured.

Rafe's mouth dropped open. "Awful to look at? Lord,

Cady, you're the most gorgeous thing I've ever seen." He put his lips to her belly. "And I love this best of all. Swim with me, Cady."

Cady couldn't take her eyes off her naked husband as he led her into the water. The freedom of swimming in the ocean without clothes and with Rafe was such an exhilarating experience that she shouted out loud as he swam under her and surfaced next to her. They frolicked like children.

When Rafe carried her out of the water, he didn't stop at the blanket but kept going right into the house, then to the bedroom. "You've had too much sun," he mumbled into her neck as he followed her down onto the bed. "Besides, I have something to tell you." He leaned on his elbows over her body. "I never would have said anything if you hadn't said you loved me, Cady. You know you told me that when we first married, and it made me so happy. But I was afraid to accept that you really did. After all, you were only eighteen when I married you." He held her face between his two hands. "I loved you so much before I left your bedroom, that first day we met, and I kept loving you more and more after we were married. After a few years I had the feeling that you were growing tired of me."

"Bruno kept telling me stories about you...and Durra...and women." Cady felt as though she were floating.

"I know that now. I didn't then. I stayed away from you, hoping that you wouldn't want to leave me if I gave you enough freedom. But I'll tell you, Cady, I wanted you with me every second of every day. I love you so much that if I start now and tell you for a thousand years, I'll still come up short."

"Me, too." Cady felt a tear roll down her cheek. He had said the words, reaffirming their lifelong commitment to each other.

"You're all I have ever wanted, all I'll ever want." Rafe lay down at her side, cuddling her to him until the inevitable heat built between them. The gentle explosion rocked them both, awing them with its scope.

Six months later Rafe Nesbitt Densmore was born, thrilling Cady with his fluff of dark brown hair and his shoe-button blue eyes.

After the birth, Rafe pressed his face into her breast and whispered to her over and over again, "I love you, Cady. I love you." The damp glitter of his eyes told her that nothing could tear them apart.

She had tread softly on Rafe's dreams, and he had made all hers come true.

DON'T MISS THESE TITLES IN THE SECOND CHANCE AT LOVE SERIES

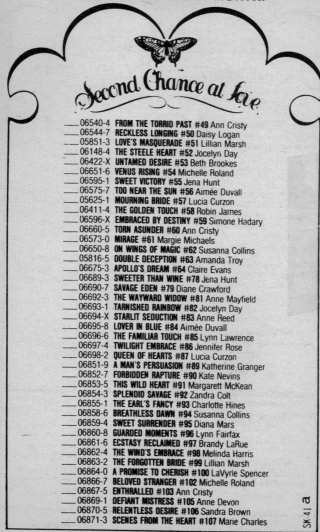

All of the above titles are $1.75 per copy except where noted

Available at your local bookstore or return this form to:

SECOND CHANCE AT LOVE
Book Mailing Service
P.O. Box 690, Rockville Centre, NY 11571

Please send me the titles checked above. I enclose _____
Include $1.00 for postage and handling if one book is ordered; 50¢ per book for
two or more books. California, Illinois, New York and Tennessee residents please add
sales tax.

NAME _____

ADDRESS _____

CITY _____ STATE/ZIP _____
(allow six weeks for delivery)

SK-41b